Shakespeare
Undead

Also by Lori Handeland

Shakespeare Undead

Lori Handeland

St. Martin's Griffin   New York

This is a work of fiction. All of the characters, organizations, and events portrayed in this novel are either products of the author's imagination or are used fictitiously.

www.stmartins.com

ISBN 978-0-312-64152-8

First Edition: June 2010

10 9 8 7 6 5 4 3 2 1

Acknowledgments

Jennifer Enderlin—for sharing the title of this book during a breakfast in Washington, D.C. And the rest, as they say, is history.

Thanks, Jen!

Author's Note

Who was the Dark Lady of Shakespeare's sonnets? Those works of exquisite beauty that portray tormented desire, temptation, betrayal, and eternal love for a woman with dark eyes, raven hair, dun skin—and a husband. Many have theorized, but no one knows the truth.

Until now . . .

Shakespeare Undead

Chapter One

"Though this be madness, yet there is method in 't."
                                                —*Hamlet* (Act II, scene 2)

London, Autumn—1592

What was left of the man shambled into the dark alley, and I followed. I had little choice.

I am a *chasseur,* a hunter. What I hunt are those whose souls are controlled by another. I call them the *tibonage.*

You'd call them zombies.

Yes, they exist. All over the damn place.

Tonight, they existed in Southwark, and it was my job to make sure they didn't crack open someone's head and make a feast of their brains. The only way to do that was to kill them first.

The tibonage dragged his feet through the muck, intent on something in the distance. This is the nature of zombies. They are raised for a reason; they have a mission. Nothing will stop them from completing it.

Except me.

"Halt!" I shouted. The tibonage didn't even glance my way.

Definitely on a mission. Weren't we all?

I hurried after, careful to remain far enough away that the zombie couldn't spin and grab me. Although they're the walking dead, the tibonage are faster than one might think, and if prevented from completing their assignments, they fight like baited bears.

As soon as I came within a sword's length, I planted my feet and drew my weapon, wincing when the slick slide sliced through the still air. The tibonage froze, then slowly he turned.

I should have cut off his head right then. If I had, I never would have seen his face in the silvery glow of the moon.

Instead, I whispered, "Chalmers?"

One of our servants. He'd died only last week.

Hair still well-groomed, nails too, skin a wee bit gray but not terribly so. There wasn't a hole in him anywhere there shouldn't be. I'd have thought him alive if it weren't for the smell. I wrinkled my nose.

He was dead all right.

The zombie yanked me close, his teeth clacking together inches from my nose. I dropped the sword and shoved against his chest. Beneath my palms, his skin squirmed. A maggot peeked past the collar of his dusty doublet and winked.

"Erk!" I shrieked, and jerked my hands away. This only allowed the tibonage to pull me even closer.

"Br-br-br," he chanted, in between the clicking of teeth. "Mmmm," he growled low. "Mmmm."

He obviously hadn't had his daily supply of *br-br-br*—

"Brains," I snapped, annoyed at both myself for not killing him and him for being unable to articulate a simple word. "If you could *say* brains, you might actually possess enough of them to get some."

Talking to a zombie was almost as foolish as wrestling one. I'm strong, but zombies are stronger. I'm not sure why.

Perhaps there was something in the way they were raised that gave them certain powers. For instance, remaining unharmed through everything but decapitation and fire. That, combined with superior strength, meant the only advantage I had was that *my* brains could be used for something other than stuffing between my ears.

I lifted my knee, fast and hard. If his choked shriek was any indication, his balls now had an intimate acquaintance with his throat.

He let me go. He didn't have much choice. He was on the ground, clutching his privates and keening. I rescued my sword, then I returned Chalmers to God.

The man had always been overly tall, so even on his knees his head was nearly level with mine. As a result, when he burst into ashes, I got a faceful. Then I couldn't see.

Which was the only excuse for what happened next. When the shuffle that sounded behind me was followed by a touch on my shoulder, I reacted. Two hands on the hilt of my sword, I swung, and I connected.

Blood washed the ashes from my face.

"Oh," I whispered. "N-n-n-no."

I sounded like a zombie. But I wasn't, and neither was the man who tumbled to the muck-strewn cobblestones. If he had been, such a wound would not have bothered him in the least.

I fell to my knees as my victim's eyes fluttered closed, and I sat there until the blood from the slice in his neck stopped flowing. Then I laid my palm against his chest, but the heart beneath no longer beat; his skin had already cooled.

Should I search out the authorities and attempt to explain?

A half laugh, half sob escaped my throat. "Excuse me, there is a dead man in the alley. But I didn't mean to slit his throat, sirrah. Oh no, I meant to cut off his head."

I lifted trembling fingers, meaning to rub at the pain in the center of my forehead, but when I saw the blood I let my arm drop back to my side.

"Who would have thought he could have so much blood in him?" I whispered. "Will I ever be able to wash my hands clean?"

The stranger was dead. The only way to bring him back would be to ferret out someone who could raise him. But then he would be a zombie—his soul in thrall to another. I doubted this man, whoever he was, would thank me for that.

No, better to leave him where he lay. At least his soul was already with God.

Chapter Two

"Cry 'Havoc,' and let slip the dogs of war."
—Julius Caesar (Act III, scene 1)

The evening began the same as so many others. Will tried to write. He didn't have much luck.

Because his writing of late was not writing at all. Of late, his writing was mostly staring.

Which was why he'd begun staying at the Rose Theatre after his final curtain. Being alone in his living quarters from midnight to dawn, with only a full quill and an empty page for company, had nearly driven him mad. Though many would say he had been traveling that path for some time now.

"Master Shakespeare!"

Will glanced up from the table, happy for a diversion. Any diversion. "What is it, Edmond?"

A few people still milled about the theater, but many had left. Most of the candles had been blown out, and shadows reigned. Even if he hadn't already recognized the squat, fantastically round silhouette weaving toward him at an alarming pace, Will would have known the voice, which was high and childlike despite the man's bulk.

Will blinked as Edmond got closer. Was he attempting to run? Edmond never ran. When he did, church bells rang of their own accord, and small buildings tumbled down.

Something dreadful must have happened to cause Edmond not only to move faster than a three-legged mule but entice him to drink so much he could barely remain on his feet.

Not that Edmond didn't drink. On the contrary, he did so daily and to excess, but his most important responsibility was to remain at the Rose through the night, on guard against any who might harm it. Therefore, he usually waited to imbibe until midday.

As the man stumbled closer, and the floor beneath them wobbled, Will noticed something amiss. Edmond had a crack in his head, and blood poured down his face.

Will's stomach clenched sickeningly, and he had to look away for an instant or embarrass himself. But he was a strong man—if the term *man* was taken loosely enough—and he managed to keep himself under control.

"What has happened?" Will asked. "Did you take a fall?"

Instead of answering, Edmond weaved left, then right, then dropped straight forward like a downed tree. Will had no time to get out of the way, no time to do anything but grab Edmond, lift him bodily, then set him upright.

"Marry," Will muttered, glancing around to make certain no one had seen him perform that inhuman feat. Edmond had to weigh nigh on twenty stone. By rights, the man should have crushed Will like a bug.

Praise the saints no one was about, and Edmond was too drunk to remember. Even now he swayed, eyes closed against the steady stream of blood that washed down his forehead and dripped off the end of his nose.

"Edmond!" Will gave him a sharp shake. Droplets flew, spattering against Will's doublet. One struck his chin. The scent drifted upward, and suddenly Will's teeth itched.

Right then he nearly broke the vow he'd made so long ago. Would have, if the man's eyes had not snapped open and stared into his.

"Sir!" Edmond straightened and stepped back, tripping over his own feet and nearly falling again. However, when Will reached out to help, Edmond cringed.

"Beshrew me," Will cursed. He was usually much better at acting human than this.

He thought about puppies and lambs, just-sprung flowers and saplings, blue skies, fluffy clouds, and the bright, blinding light of the sun—anything to make the scent and the sight of Edmond's blood fade from his mind.

It didn't work.

Will would never forget the smell, the texture, the ruby red sheen— Ah hell, be honest. No matter how often he drank wine, he would never forget the exquisite *flavor* of blood.

But he *could* control himself. Sometimes it just took a while.

Eventually, Will wiped that single droplet from his chin and made use of the strength he'd acquired over centuries of un-life to force the howling monster within him back down. The beast subsided at last, though there was grumbling and arguing and pain. There always was.

Will spun, and Edmond promptly fell on his arse. The floor gave with a sharp crack. "Sorry, sir," Edmond murmured.

"Oh, get up!" Will ordered. Coddling the man wasn't working. "Tell me what happened, and be quick."

Edmond lumbered to his feet. Something in Will's eyes had frightened him, but he still took orders better than most. Edmond could no more refuse to do what he was told than he could give up his daily portion of ale.

Will expected the usual tale of woe. Edmond had played cards and lost. He had not broken his fast for two weeks, yet he'd gained two stone. A woman had scorned him. Such tragedies happened quite often with Edmond, and usually resulted in just this type of behavior. But always *after* his duty to the Rose was complete.

"I saw a dead man walking, sir."

Will nearly fell over himself. "A what?"

"A dead man, he was."

"And—and—" Will cleared his throat, then tried to speak once more. "H-h-how did you know this?"

"The dead have a certain look."

Will ran his hand over his face. Some did.

"Hair grown long and . . ." Edmond wiggled his fat fingers by his head, giving the impression of worms instead of hair.

"Unkempt?" Will supplied.

Edmond clapped his hands together beneath his third chin. "My Lord, you always know the perfect word."

"Not lately," Will muttered. At Edmond's curious expression, he shook his head. "Go on," he urged, though he knew all too well what Edmond would say.

"His fingernails were . . ." Edmond frowned as he stared at his own, which were dirty and yellowed.

"Long?" Will asked.

"Some." Edmond continued to frown. "Others were broken and filthy, as if he'd clawed his way out of the grave. And his toes—" Edmond shuddered.

"Aye?" Will encouraged. "What about his toes?"

"His feet were bare, and the nails of his toes tapped against the stones of the street. The noise, sir, 'twas horrible."

"I can imagine," Will said, though he didn't have to. He'd heard it himself, thousands of times before, with his own overly keen ears.

"The flesh was gray and pocked," Edmond continued, "his eyes empty of life. What clothing remained on his person hung in tatters and was covered in dust and dirt. The parts of his—" Edmond paused, pursed his lips, then whispered conspiratorially, "nakedness that could be seen had sores and—" Edmond winced. "Bugs. Nigh put me off my dinner, it did."

"I'd like to see something that could put *you* off your dinner," said a new voice. Laughter followed.

Will glanced over his shoulder. Several of the stage crew had become bored with their dice game and now listened with obvious amusement to Edmond's account.

"Make yourself useful," Will said. "Find the man a cloth to staunch his wound."

Instead of scattering like the vultures they were, one of them held out a grimy handkerchief. Will snatched it up and set it against Edmond's head, careful not to touch anything but the cloth. He had fantastic control, but there was no need to poke at the beast.

"How'd you get that knock on yer noggin'?" the nearest man, Arthur Cartwright, asked.

"I thought the gentleman was ill," Edmond said. "I wanted to help."

Will patted Edmond's arm. He might be a drunk, but he was a sweet drunk. Will had known that even before he'd caught the scent of the man's blood.

Sweeeet.

Fie! Will scolded himself. *Focus on the problem and forget everything else!*

Easier thought than accomplished, especially with blood all over Edmond's face, neck, and now hands.

"'Twas a trap, weren't it? The Jack robbed ye, he did. After he slammed yer head—" Arthur paused. "Where did he slam yer head?"

"Against the wall of a church!" Edmond's voice was aghast. "He was obviously a fiend from hell."

"Obviously," Will murmured. "Pray continue. What then?"

"He smacked me again and again as if he were tryin' to open my skull, and all the while he gurgled a word I had some trouble makin' out."

"What word?" Will asked, but he knew.

"I could have sworn, sir"—Edmond paused, lowering the cloth from his head so he could meet Will's eyes—"that he was chantin' 'brains.'"

Aye, Will thought, *he was.*

"His teeth were snappin' together as if he'd eat his way right through my skull. Then he started makin' yummy sounds."

"Yummy sounds," Will repeated.

"Mmmm," Edmond said, rubbing his stomach for emphasis. "Mmmmmmmmm!"

Laughter erupted again, and Edmond flinched. His shoulders hunched as he lifted the now-red cloth and hid his face from their mirth.

"Why would anyone want to crack open yer head and eat yer brains?" Arthur asked. "Can't be much of a meal."

Everyone snickered. Except Edmond.

And Will.

Will wanted to put a stop to the harassment, but he needed the distraction. He soothed his conscience by assuring himself he would send a doctor to tend Edmond's head.

Just as soon as he found the zombie.

Will slipped backward as the onlookers tightened their circle around the bleeding man.

"Ye see a lot of dead folks?" Arthur asked.

Edmond considered. "Never afore today."

Hallelujah! Will thought. Maybe there was only one.

Except there was *never* only one.

"Ye didn't see any today either," Arthur continued. "Someone tried to rob ye, fool. They banged yer head against a building."

"Church!" Edmond insisted stubbornly.

"Church," Arthur agreed. "And when they found ye had nothing to offer but evil-smelling breath, they smacked ye again and left ye to bleed."

Confusion spread over Edmond's face. He was starting to doubt. "Pure evil I saw in his eyes. He was not human."

"Neither are you."

More laughter erupted, drowning out Edmond's response, as Will reached the front entrance and became one with the night.

He knew how things would progress whilst he was away. The others would attempt to convince Edmond that he had not seen what he had, and by morning, when the man awoke with a headache to rival the ones he received from too much ale, he would believe them.

Human beings were very good at rationalizing. Will wished

he still had the ability. Unfortunately, he was one of the things humans rationalized about.

He could attempt to explain Edmond's attack as being made by a sick man desperately needing coin. If it hadn't been for the word *brains.*

And the yummy sounds.

Simply put, what Edmond had seen on the streets of London was a zombie. Will should know. In times past, he was the one who had raised them.

His feet led him to the nearest church, where he checked the stone for traces of Edmond's blood but found none. Which meant there was none to be found. If Will was good at one other thing, besides writing and acting, it was catching the scent or the sight of blood.

He moved on. He very nearly passed right by Southwark Cathedral without pausing. In Will's mind, a cathedral and a church were two very different things, and Southwark Cathedral was very different indeed. The oldest place of worship in London, the site had been home to some form of church since A.D. 606. Rumor had it that there'd been a pagan Roman temple there before that. As Will had been here when the Romans came, he knew the rumor to be true.

However, as he hurried by, gaze flicking from alley to street and back again, searching for the telltale shamble that signaled zombie, he caught the scent of blood.

He found splashes of red all over the place—on the cornerstone, the cobblestones, then in a weaving trail toward the Rose.

Will checked the street again. He expected to find no one else about but him, perhaps a thief or two. Instead, the long shadow of a man spread across the road three buildings up.

He walked the way zombies walk, as though all of the out-houses in England were full, and he badly needed one empty.

Will hurried in that direction. The zombie was up to no good. They always were. Such creatures would mindlessly continue to follow the orders of the one who made them. Will could chop off their arms, their legs. Hell, he could chop them in half, and both halves would continue to drag themselves toward their ultimate goal. To stop a zombie with a sword, one had to lop off its head.

Not that Will had ever done so. The creatures *he'd* made had turned to dust on the battlefields of England, Rome, and Scotland for the Henries, Julius Caesar, and Macbeth. Will had raised them; they'd fought; he'd been paid. When the war was won, those left were dispatched, but not by him.

He was sorry for the raising now. So many had died. But when he'd been newly made, with a bright, endless future but no funds, the idea had seemed like a good one. It was only later that he saw how very bad an idea it was. Ideas were so often like that.

Will had an affinity for the dead. The talent was not something he'd gained upon becoming one of them, but something he'd had since he was born.

The first time.

Will had been labeled an insane child, a lunatic youth. Talking to empty air was not something one did in the years before the birth of Christ, or in the centuries thereafter either. Explaining that he saw dead people, could talk to them, and they talked back, had been a foolish choice on his part.

Will had managed to avoid being burned for a witch, but it had been a very close thing. Forsooth, joining the ranks of the undead when he was six-and-twenty had been a relief.

He no longer had to hide anything but himself from the light.

He was able to fit in amongst the living so much better now that he was dead. He need only behave "normally," for the most part, during the darkest hours, and humans were not at their best then. They were meant to walk in the light.

Add to this Will's profession—being a player was the perfect occupation for one such as he. Actors were known to be strange. Amongst them, Will was no more odd than any other.

And if he spoke to empty rooms and deserted corners, those in his company believed the habit a quirk of his genius. He merely spoke to his characters, practiced dialogue, perfected stage movements before he wrote them down.

In such beliefs they were largely correct. Will *did* speak to his characters. However, sometimes his characters talked back.

He'd known Henry—all of them—along with Richard, Macbeth, and his insane wife too. Now that they were dead, each and every one wanted him to tell their stories.

He didn't mind, but he had his own stories to set on the page as well. He just hadn't been able to do so of late. Not only had his muse gone silent, but his cursed ghosts too. He had begun to wonder if any of them—muse or ghosts—would ever come back and what he would do if they did not. Perhaps walk straight into the morning sun.

Despite the darkness, Will saw the zombie without any trouble. This was not the same creature that had tried to crack Edmond's head like an egg but one so new it could have been taken for the living. Because of the shambling and the moaning, the zombie could easily be labeled a plague victim, probably would be by most, but Will knew better.

As he hurried to catch up, a figure detached from the shadows. Will tensed, expecting it to move like a zombie, groan like a zombie, attempt murder like a zombie. Instead, the new arrival seemed to float, graceful as a swan on the royal pond, slim as one of the reeds that lined the shores.

Black cap, black doublet, black breeches, even black boots—small wonder he hadn't detected the boy. The lad blended into the night better than Will did.

Will opened his mouth to call out, to stop the slight, slim figure from getting too close. But the telltale swish of a sword leaving its scabbard had Will snapping his mouth shut so quickly he narrowly missed eating his own tongue.

Reaching for his own sword as he stepped into the alley, Will cursed when he didn't find it. He'd left the weapon at the Rose.

Though most young men always went out with both a sword *and* a dagger, especially in Southwark, Will did not. He had no need. Killing Will Shakespeare was beyond the capabilities of most humans.

Will did have his dagger on his belt, more for show than anything else, but he didn't bother to retrieve it. Beheading is much harder than one might think. To cleave a head from the shoulders, a dagger would be of little use.

But Will's bare hands were a deadly weapon. Though he was an actor and a writer by trade, and therefore did not *appear* strong, Will was almost as much of a monster as the one he'd followed here. Wresting free the head would be a simple enough task.

Hideous and disgusting. But simple.

However, upon entering the alley, Will discovered he needn't have worried. Ashes as thick as a locust plague floated through the air.

Will was so impressed that the boy had already dispatched the corpse, he strode forward and put his hand on the lad's shoulder. He should have known better. Anyone who'd been confronted by the walking dead would be understandably overwrought. The child was no exception.

He spun on nimble feet, slicing Will's neck from ear to ear.

Chapter Three

"I hold the world but as the world . . . A stage, where every man must play a part; and mine a sad one."

—*The Merchant of Venice* (Act I, scene 1)

I ran across the rooftop as if Cerberus nipped at my heels.

Dear God, I'd killed someone!

Many would say I'd killed before, but I did not believe that. When I beheaded a tibonage, I was *saving* them. Besides, how can you kill something that is already dead?

However, the stranger in the alley—

Him, I had killed.

If I was caught, I'd be hanged or worse, and I couldn't allow that to happen. Not just because I preferred my neck exactly the way it was, but I had a calling. There were only a chosen few with my knowledge and skills. If I stopped doing the duty I had been charged with, England was doomed.

I had been taught to hunt by my nurse, my nanny, my *nou-nou*. She had once been the greatest chasseur in Haiti.

After she was brought there from the depths of Africa when she was fifteen, Papa had bought Nounou as a gift for my twelfth birthday to smooth over the loss of my mother in childbed a few months before.

Nounou had become my greatest friend. I missed her as deeply as I would miss the arm with which I wielded my sword.

She had been gone nigh on a year. Nevertheless, every time I left my room to hunt, I ached with her loss.

Despite her advancing age, Nounou had refused to allow me to hunt alone. Therefore, I had been close enough to see the blow that had killed her but too far away to do anything about it.

The zombies we had fought that night had been strong and well armed. Despite the clang of steel on steel, I'd heard her soft gasp, turned, and seen her fall, run through by the damned walking dead.

I slashed my way through those that were left; ashes became as thick as dust on a country road. But by the time I had reached her, she was gone. Not a word of good-bye, no time to hold her hand as she slipped away, no chance to say I loved her.

For that, and so much more, I would spend my life ridding the earth of the fiends that had taken Nounou from me.

I reached the manor house and slid into the garden, then climbed the trellis to the balcony outside my room.

Who had the man I'd just killed been?

Distracted with thoughts of the handsome stranger—I hadn't seen much, but what I'd seen had been quite lovely—I allowed my boots to thump against the balcony as I landed.

A knock sounded on the door. "Katherine!"

"Ods bodkins," I muttered. "Most days she cannot hear a word that I speak, yet one single tread of my foot awakens her."

I tugged off my cap, and my unfashionably dark hair tumbled past my waist. After kicking off the offending boots, I shoved them, along with the bloody sword, beneath the bed before I leaped under the sheets and coverlet. At almost the same instant the door opened, and my husband's old nurse strode in.

Thin as a crow and stupid as a sheep, Nurse appeared as ancient as some of the stones in the Tower of London. I no longer needed a nurse; I was of an age to need a lady's maid. But my husband needed a spy.

Hence the nurse.

At least she knew how to fashion my hair and could double as a lady's maid had I ever the need for one. As it was, I never went out. That she was aware of.

I had no idea why my husband trusted me so little. Reginald could not know that I left the house each night. I'd learned quite quickly that he responded to misbehavior immediately and cruelly. Therefore, if I was still allowed the freedom to get out of the house at all, he did not know that I had done so.

Perhaps his living in Virginia for a good portion of the year made him believe I needed watching over.

Or perhaps he was a lunatic.

Luckily for me and my calling, Reginald seemed unaware that Nurse was almost as deaf as she was dumb, and her age meant she slept often and well. Most nights, I was on the streets and hunting by nine.

"What was that noise?" Nurse hurried to the side of the bed.

While awake, she heard thuds better than words, so I'd taken great care not to make them. Until tonight. I must have arrived as Nurse was returning from one of her frequent trips to the garderobe.

Sheets drawn to my chin, I behaved as if I'd been woken from sleep. "What say you? Noise? I heard nothing."

Nurse, whose face was as emaciated as the rest of her, widened her large, milky blue eyes in surprise. "That cannot be. Two thuds, I swear. One." She stomped a foot. "And two."

She stomped again as if I did not know what a thud sounded like, and beneath the bed, my sword rattled.

I pretended to have a coughing fit. I needn't have bothered; Nurse noticed nothing amiss. She could hear little over the sound of her own voice, which never quieted.

"Ach." She put her long, bony hands against her sunken cheeks. "I have heard tales of other nurses' charges sneaking out at night, getting into all sorts of mischief. But, then, those nurses have young ones to watch, and I . . ." She smiled widely, revealing the six brown teeth she still possessed. "I have you. I am so fortunate. I thank the good Lord daily that my dear Master Dymond thought of me when he needed someone to wa—"

She broke off. I lifted a brow. "Yes, *dear* nurse? He needed someone to . . . ?"

Nurse let her hands fall to her sharply pointed hips. "How now? What is this? Ye have not braided yer hair. 'Twill be a tangle come the morn. Let me." She motioned for me to sit up. "Anon."

"I cannot, good nurse."

For if I do, you will see that I have been out hunting and tell Reginald since you have been sent to wa— me.

I loathed being spied upon, but since Nurse was a terrible spy, I managed. However, if Reginald discovered what I'd been doing, he would send Nurse away and employ someone with more brains than the average village idiot.

"I am so tired of late." I made my voice weak and wispy. If I said so myself, I was a very good actress. Quite fortunate since I had so many to fool.

As a lonely, only child, I'd often pretended to be who I wasn't—King Henry back when he was the handsomest prince in Christendom, Sir Thomas the martyr, the royal Tudor princesses, and eventually the Virgin Queen. Oh, how I wished I were her! Particularly the virgin part. Sometimes still, when I was alone and lonely, I pretended.

"Tired?" Nurse repeated. "Tired?"

The lamplight flashed off her kerchief, which resembled the sail of a midsized ship, while Nurse herself resembled the mast. When the woman went to market, her headdress was so large she knocked over the produce every time she turned.

In truth, she brought along a servant to pick up after her. The sight of Nurse and her boy bearing down sent merchants scurrying in all directions to hide their most expensive wares before they were ruined.

"Saints be praised!" Nurse cried, and when she cried, ears wept. "You are with child at last."

Nausea rolled over me. God's teeth. Thus far I'd managed to avoid that tragedy.

Not that I didn't care for children. What I didn't care for was Reginald.

I had at first. He'd wooed and won me with pretty words and false promises. It wasn't until the morning after our marriage that I realized he'd married me for my money.

Or rather, for Papa's money.

My dear father had bought Reginald for me in the same way he'd bought Nounou. The distant relative of an earl, Reginald had "good blood." With his pedigree and Papa's funds, the two believed a title was in Reginald's future.

I had been furious to discover they had plotted the rest of my life behind my back without my knowledge or consent, as if I didn't have the intelligence to know what was good for me.

I knew now, and it definitely wasn't Reginald.

I had made my unhappiness known. That was the first time Reginald locked me in my room.

It wasn't the last.

As a condition of our marriage contract, Reginald spent a majority of the year across the sea in Virginia, attempting to make the tobacco plantation my father had bought there prosper. Once the plantation began to turn a tidy profit, Papa would do his best to secure Reginald a barony.

I was completely indifferent to becoming Lady Whoever. But I'd understood very quickly that despite what he'd said while "courting" me, Reginald cared only for himself. I was the means to his title and the mother of his heirs. Period.

Reginald had been gone several months, and I'd known I wasn't carrying soon after he'd left. That Nurse had conveniently forgotten this fact was not surprising. Sometimes she forgot the date.

As I'd never been regular in my courses, the lack of one since did not disturb me. I'd only have been disturbed if I hadn't had one at all.

Despite my knowledge of the lie, I murmured languidly, "Perhaps, I am, good nurse, perhaps."

Anything to make the woman *go*.

"At last!" Nurse shouted. "I feared ye'd never get with child. Not that it is completely your fault, mind you. What with the master in the wilderness most of the time."

"Praise God," I muttered. Not that "the master" didn't do his best to make up for the nights he was away whenever he was at home.

I shuddered at the memory, and Nurse snatched a blanket from the chest at the foot of my bed, then tucked me in. "Best not to mention that," she murmured.

Nurse might be slow-witted, but she had the instincts of the animals she resembled. She knew better than to poke a wild beast, which was what Reginald could become if he believed he was being blamed for anything at all.

"Still," Nurse continued, "the master will be so pleased. May I be the one to tell him?" She took a quick, shallow breath—the better to keep talking with the least amount of silence. "No, that would not be proper. Perhaps you should write him." She shook her head. "Not yet. Make sure you do not miscarry. He would be heartbroken. I would be. Not that such will happen. No. Be not afraid, child." She clasped her birdlike claws beneath her weak but pointed chin. "Oh, to have a little one in the house once more."

Would the woman never cease her prattle? My head would soon begin to ache. If I hadn't been wearing black breeches and a man's black shirt beneath the coverlet, I would have gotten up and led her to the door. Instead, I snapped, "Nurse!"

As if she hadn't heard—she probably hadn't—she continued to talk. "A boy or a girl? A boy methinks. For the barony. Might ye be carrying a boy? Hard to know until ye begin to carry high or low. I know a wisewoman who could come lay on her hands." She made the motion in front of her own nonexistent belly of palming the fullness. "She'd tell ye what she saw within."

Since shouting had done no good, I resorted to pantomime, waving my free hand at the door, then laying its back against my forehead as if exhausted. I wasn't even acting anymore.

"Of course, child. Ye need yer sleep. But oh!" Nurse clapped her palms against her pale, drawn cheeks. "Would it not be wonderful if the babe resembled his father?"

I stifled a wince. Reginald was not an attractive man. Certainly, he had fashionably fair hair, but precious little of it, and blue eyes. However, they squinted far too much and gave him the appearance of an overworked clerk. His nose was also unfortunate, and the idea of such a bulbous appendage appearing in the center of an innocent child's face—along with the hairy mole at nose's end—brought tears to my eyes.

Not that I was of the fashion, as Reginald took every opportunity to point out once we were married. Dark of hair and eye and even skin, when beauty was defined by how fair and blond and light-eyed one might be, I was also slim and boyish—a good thing for the hunt, but not so for a ball gown. To make mine fit correctly, my great-aunt Margaret had insisted I stuff the bodice with scraps from the makings of the dress itself.

When Reginald had taken off my clothes that first night, he had shaken in fury at what he found beneath. Or rather, what he *hadn't* found.

I closed my eyes against the memory. I knew that doing my wifely duty was not supposed to be pleasant, but I'd still been stunned at how *un*pleasant it was.

Believing me nearly asleep—I should really go on the stage, would have if I were truly the boy I pretended to be— Nurse bustled toward the door. "That's it, child, close yer eyes. 'Tis sleep ye need. Ye will feel better come the morn. Of that I am cert—"

The latch clicked, muffling Nurse's voice midword, although I could still hear her talking to herself in the hall. The murmur faded as she moved farther and farther from my door.

I threw back the covers, leaped to my feet, and yanked my breeches down to my ankles. I nearly tripped and fell on my face when the door began to open.

"Would ye like something to eat? I'm sure that bairn in your belly must be hungry." Nurse chuckled.

I was in such a great rush to get the covers over myself, I poked my thumb into my eye. Sometimes I swore Nurse wasn't as dumb or as deaf as she appeared. Then there were the times I knew she was.

"Prithee, only sleep!" I shouted. Why had I even hinted at a child? Now I would hear of little else.

"All right," Nurse grumbled, backing away. "Ye do not have t' shout." The door closed.

I waited. Then I waited a bit more, eyes fixed on the door, ears straining for the lightest footstep.

There were days I thought I would run mad. In this house I never found a single moment's peace. The only thing that soothed my mind and kept me sane were the nights I spent hunting for zombies in the bowels of London.

At last, when I heard a sharp snore from beyond, I glanced at the balcony. I wouldn't sleep tonight. Whenever I closed my eyes, all I would see was the face of the stranger I had killed. The only way to make up for the life I had taken was to save other lives, and the only way to do that was to kill the tibonage. Lately, there were far too many of them out there.

Within minutes I'd slipped from the bed, cleaned off my sword, then gone over the balcony and into the night.

Chapter Four

"A man can die but once."
—*Henry IV Part II* (Act III, scene 2)

Will came back to the world slowly. First his hearing returned. Shouts and cries caused him to remember where he lay.

Southwark. He'd best be up and about before someone killed him. Again.

Next came his sense of smell. Blood. His own. Water. Stale and warm. Garbage. A rat.

The boy.

He was no longer there, but his scent remained, a strange mixture of sweet sweat and flowers. Perhaps the lad spent his days as an apprentice to a gardener.

Will opened his eyes. Darkness hovered all around, and for an instant he thought he might truly be dead. Then his sight sharpened; clouds had moved in, dimming both the moon and the stars. A hint of rain—this was England after all—blew in on the breeze.

Lastly, he felt the pain. He lay on the damp, hard, cold cobblestones. Not that his body wasn't harder and colder,

but try dying on them. Even though he'd come back to life as
he always did, dying *hurt*.

Every damn time.

Will felt his neck. The only remnant of his throat being
slit was a thin, almost healed line and blood all over the
place.

The alley was empty; a chill wind whistled through.
Moisture glittered on the cobblestones. Autumn hovered
at the edge of night.

A stealthy shuffle sounded from the street, and Will got
slowly to his feet. If anyone saw him like this, there'd be more
questions than he cared to answer. So he tore a strip of his
linen shirt free and wound it around his neck like a bandage.

A covered wound and a lot of blood could be explained.
No wound and a lot of blood would make people wonder
just who, and how many, he'd killed.

Will moved forward, planning to exit the far side of the
alley from the one he'd entered and ask about, try to discover if anyone was acquainted with the boy. But before he
could reach the lighter gray of the opening, the form of a
man blocked the distant sheen of the moon.

"Uurgh," he said.

"Zounds," Will muttered. How many of the cursed beings
were out there?

The creature started toward him. Before Will could stop
himself, he took a pace back and bumped into another.

"Glurk," it said.

Spinning, Will reached for his dagger. It wouldn't do a bit
of good, but he had to have something.

The woman was large, probably thirteen stone and solid
muscle. When still alive, she had likely been the wife of a

farmer or perhaps a stonemason's bride. Though her skin was gray—the grave has that effect—her face was unlined and had once been quite pretty.

Before her left eye rotted out.

Will stepped away, and once more bumped into the first. What this one had been before he'd become a zombie, besides alive, was difficult to determine. His clothes had fallen off. His body had holes where holes should never be. He still possessed most of his teeth, which only made the way he opened and shut, opened and shut his mouth more horrifying. Those teeth clicked together as if he were freezing to death. Perhaps he had.

He opened his arms for an embrace, but Will knew better. Zombies did not feel emotion. They only understood what they'd been ordered to do, and they certainly hadn't been ordered to hug Will Shakespeare.

Will ducked and stepped to the side. He could only assume that at the same moment, the female clapped her arms together in an attempt to catch, then kill, him. Instead, the two caught each other.

By the time Will had straightened, they were rolling on the slick cobblestones, growling and kicking, biting and hitting. Flesh flew, hair too, the thuds of body on body sickening. Because zombies felt no pain, this might go on for days.

Though he knew better, nevertheless Will shouted, "Stop!"

Since he had not made them, they did not listen. He attempted to reach in and snatch the man in one hand, the woman in the other, but they bit him!

It was a myth that the bite of a zombie would turn the bitten undead. Indeed, it turns them *dead*.

There is something in a zombie's rotted, rancid mouth

like poison that causes the bite to fester. Within days, the afflicted occupies his grave. But contrary to popular legend, he will not rise from it without help.

Such an infection would not bother Will, but still he did not care for being bitten. He'd only just recovered from being killed.

Will tried again to part the two before they separated each other's heads from their bodies. He didn't want them forever dead. He needed to know what their orders were and who had done the ordering. Since they couldn't speak beyond the constant chant for *br-br-br*— and a little gibberish, he must follow them, which would be damned difficult once their ashes twirled on the breeze.

Before Will got a good grasp, twin thumps from behind made him spin. Expecting more zombies, Will gaped at the sight of the boy. How had he gotten so close without Will detecting him? Will could hear the pulse of blood through veins. Yet this child had crept near enough that he could have swiped *Will's* head from his shoulders with the sword he now brandished.

The lad took one look at Will and gaped as well. And why wouldn't he? The last time the child had seen Will Shakespeare he'd been bleeding to death.

"Fool," Will muttered. He had not lived so many lifetimes by being stupid. But there was always a first time, and if he wasn't careful, there would be a last time too. He was going to have to come up with an explanation for being alive, and damn quickly.

The boy swung his sword in a forward arc.

Will opened his mouth to shout "No!" but it was too late. The blade clanged into the stones, shooting sparks, cleaving zombie head from zombie body once, then once more.

The lad spun through the ashes, a dancelike movement so graceful it took Will an instant to realize the blade was coming for him.

He might have been slow-witted this eve, but he was not slow-moving. Will ducked again. Forsooth, he could move faster than the human eye could see if he was of a mind to. With the blade but a wisp from his throat, Will was of a mind to.

The sword struck stone, this time against a building, not the ground, and more sparks flew. The boy muttered something in what sounded very much like French. Interesting.

Living for centuries, traveling the globe, Will had learned several languages, French among them, Latin too, but it had always been English that fascinated him.

Though in truth the child might only know French curses, he did not speak with the lower-class accent so familiar in these parts. If Will didn't know better, he'd think him of the nobility.

But Will had no occasion to ponder further, as the boy twirled and twisted, then lunged. This time Will was ready, and he snatched the sword from an unsuspecting hand.

The edge was sharp; it cut Will's palm. Blood flowed, the scent upon the breeze enticing. Will gritted his teeth as his belly clenched, and desire rushed over him like the tide.

The lad's head tilted downward, the brim of his hat shading his face. Will could not see anything beyond the perfection of one cheek and his smooth, dusky chin. Nevertheless, his stomach fluttered.

What was it about that cheek and chin that made Will want to knock the hat from the child's head and gaze upon every inch of his face? Will found himself captivated, and as always when that happened, words and phrases flickered through his mind.

Shall I compare thee to a summer's day? Thou art more lovely and—

"Go ahead."

The words disappeared. Would they ever come back?

Will returned his attention to the boy, whose voice had not yet changed but remained high and lush, yet firm and unafraid.

"Do it!"

"You think I mean to kill you?"

A flicker of the child's dark eyes, up and then away. What eyelashes! How mortifying for the lad.

If I could write the beauty of your eyes. And in fresh numbers number all—

"You do not?"

"'Sblood," Will muttered as the rest of the phrase flew from his mind.

The lad's shoulders stiffened. He held himself tense and wary, and Will sighed. "I am not a monster." Will tossed the sword into the corner.

"What are you?" the child asked, his gaze on the bloody bandage about Will's throat.

Clenching his palm to hide the just-healed skin, Will answered, "A man."

The boy's chin went up. "I killed you."

The moon came free of the clouds, canting across the lad's face, and Will's breath went sharp and hot in his chest. He was so damn beautiful.

Mine eye hath played the painter and hath stelled thy beauty's form in table of my heart; my body is—

Will forced himself to stop. If he continued to compose

sonnets in his head, the child would take up his sword and cleave that head from Will's shoulders. Such an injury would never heal.

"You did not hurt me as badly as you thought," Will managed, unable to stop staring at the fine bones, the smooth skin, the lashes that cast silky shadows against a pristine cheek.

Whatever was wrong with him? Though many of Will's kind took human lovers of both sexes, then discarded them like dried husks when they were through, Will had never been able to do so.

Others needed the thrill of the hunt. They made a game of death. They *liked* to kill. Will's interest in such games had never been high. Not that he hadn't played them.

Boredom sets in quickly when a man lives forever. Will had been able to stave it off with his writing. The writing was the reason he'd become what he had in the first place.

Perhaps there was something amiss within him because Will's stomach had always turned as much at the thought of murder as it did at the idea of sodomy. So why did the sight of this boy's eyes and cheek, his chin and lips, make Will's loins go heavy and his hands fair itch to touch him?

"I didn't hurt you?" the boy asked.

"You didn't kill me," Will corrected. It *had* hurt.

He could tell the child did not believe him, and his next words proved it.

"I felt no heart beating in your chest; you were as cold as the stones upon which you lay."

"I was senseless," Will explained. "You were upset. I have no doubt you could not hear the beat of my heart past the thunder of your own."

Doubt crept into the child's expression. "But—"

"And losing so much blood will cause the skin to feel cold to the touch." That was something Will had learned long, long ago. If a human's skin began to chill, it was time to stop feeding.

"Any wound about the head bleeds badly," Will continued.

The boy's gaze returned to Will's stained bandage. "No one could survive how badly you bled."

"Obviously, child, I *did.*"

The lad opened his mouth, then snapped it closed. He could not deny the evidence. Will wasn't dead, as far as the boy knew, and since Will wasn't chanting *br-br-br* whilst attempting to eat the boy's brains, he wasn't a zombie. Therefore, Will had to be alive.

Will found it interesting that the youth could know of zombies and how to kill them, yet be unaware of what creature possessed the ability to raise them.

However, Will didn't plan to enlighten him. Doing so would be a good way to get his throat slit twice in one night.

He had not raised these zombies. He certainly wasn't going to die for it. Or anything else if he had his way. Will Shakespeare had a lot of writing left to do.

If he could get past the cursed abyss in his head that seemed to have swallowed every last one of his words.

"You will bear a scar," the boy said softly.

Will wouldn't, but he shrugged, and said, "There are worse things."

The lad nodded. The ashes of "worse" swirled around them right now.

"How do you know of zombies?" Will asked.

"How do you?"

The child was too belligerent for his own good. One day his master would beat him, if he hadn't already.

The thought of anyone touching the boy in violence had a growl rumbling in Will's throat and his teeth itching again. If he ever found a mark on the lad—

"I am a chasseur," the youth said, pride evident in both the word and his stance.

"A hunter?"

Surprise flickered across the lad's far too pretty face. "You speak French?"

"So do you. Where did you learn?"

"France." The way he said it, *Will* did not believe *him*.

Will inched forward, and the mixture of sweet sweat and flowers washed over him. This close he recognized the scent of roses. Will's favorite.

"What lord—" Will murmured, his hand lifting in spite of himself, "what merchant educates a gardener?"

Will heard blood swishing through veins, and he wanted it. He had not wanted anyone's blood this badly for a very long time.

His knuckles brushed a smooth, dusky cheek. The boy's breath caught, the sound pure arousal, and the tempo of his pulse quickened.

Lust flared, and Will couldn't help himself.

He kissed him.

Chapter Five

"Some rise by sin, and some by virtue fall."
—*Measure for Measure* (Act II, scene I)

The stranger kissed me, and I let him. I have no idea why. He thought me a boy, which made him . . .

I wasn't sure of the proper word. Ganymede? Sodomite? Such behavior was punishable by death though I'd never heard of the sentence actually being carried out.

Regardless of what such a person might be called, the dark stranger knew how to kiss and I— Well, I did not.

The only man who had ever touched me was Reginald, and he did not bother with kisses. I never would have thought the mere joining of lips could be so appealing.

Mouth gentle, he teased his tongue along the seam of my lips then swirled it within. Shocked, I gasped, and my bound breasts brushed his chest, catching fire despite how they itched from the bonds. I wanted him to touch them, though if he did, my secret would be out.

My secret!

I shoved; he fell back. But that one touch of my fingers against his chest, and I understood he had only moved because he wished to. Beneath the dark wool of his doublet, he was as hard as stone. I had no doubt he was hard as stone everywhere.

My usual response to such a thought would be to shudder, then brace myself against what was to come. Which was why the flush of heat, the tingling of my skin, and the heaviness deep within shocked me. Was I coming down with the plague?

I stared at the stranger, memorizing his face. After this, I would not, could not, ever see him again.

Dark hair, dark eyes, a short, dark beard shadowing his mouth and chin. Tangled in his wavy hair, a single hoop adorned one ear. I wanted to take that hoop, that ear, into my mouth and suckle.

Perhaps he saw that madness in my eyes, for he took a step toward me, hand outstretched, gaze once again upon my lips. Before he could touch me, I snatched up my sword, and I ran.

He didn't call out, didn't follow, and for that I was grateful. I wasn't sure what I'd do if he came after me. Would I kiss him, or would I kill him?

I did not go directly home. Lord only knew what might follow me there.

Instead, though I wanted nothing more than to reach my bed and find blessed, dream-filled sleep, I spent an hour leaving a false and lonely trail through alleys, up this street and down that, around a corner, over a rooftop.

When at last I climbed the trellis to my room, I barely made it onto the balcony before collapsing.

I remained where I had fallen for a good long time, then

lifted trembling fingers to my still-tingling mouth and re-lived the only kiss I'd ever known.

As I often did when sleep eluded me, I ordered a bath with the hope that the warm water might help. Unfortunately, the arrival of the water coincided with the arrival of Nurse, and the woman's chatter gave me a headache.

"Methinks you should not bathe. What if you take a chill and lose the babe?"

Since there was no babe, I wasn't concerned. I'd let Nurse believe what she would. The mythical condition would allow me to beg rest more often, and any time I could be alone was worth the lie that must eventually be revealed.

"I am far too warm to catch a chill, good nurse," I said loudly.

My face was flushed with thoughts of the stranger. I should have had the servants draw a cold bath, but that would certainly send the woman into fits.

"Ye are at that, child." She peered into my face. "Dear me! Ye have a fever."

"I do not," I snapped, and climbed into the water.

"If the master discovers ye were with child, and I did not take every care, he will—" Nurse paused, and I shot her a sharp glance. The woman never stopped talking of her own accord.

"He will what?"

"Naught," Nurse said hurriedly. "But his disappointment will break my heart."

I wondered if his disappointment might break her arm.

Though Nurse's very presence made me want to shriek until I was senseless, I did not want the woman hurt. I would have to discover a way to make the imaginary child disappear without its being the fault of Nurse or anyone else.

"I just want to bathe and sleep," I said truthfully—and loudly.

"I'll wash yer hair quickly." Nurse lowered herself laboriously to the floor next to the tub.

"No!"

"No?" Her face creased in confusion. "I always wash yer hair."

The thought of having anyone's hands on me but the stranger's made my skin crawl. How . . . odd. I'd endured Reginald's touch for three years, though it hadn't been easy. Of course, that had been before I'd been well and truly kissed.

"Not tonight," I ordered.

"Ach. Of course." Nurse climbed to her feet. "So many things will change for ye now. I remember how it was."

She left the room, closing the door behind her, leaving me to stare after, wondering what on earth she had meant.

I lay back, but the heated water did little to calm me. Instead, the lap upon my belly and breasts, between my legs, brought back the handsome stranger's embrace.

He had smelled like danger—hot, spicy—yet his skin had been deliciously chilled beneath the cloth of his doublet and shirt. *How so?* I wondered. The heat blazing through me made me entertain the thought of pressing my lips to his exquisitely cool neck, running my cheek along every inch of his skin as I drew in the scent and the taste of him.

I jerked upright, sending water onto the floor. I'd been

running my palm over my breasts, stroking myself there, then much lower. As a result, my breath came in sharp spurts, and the hot water felt almost cool along my fiery skin.

"He is a sorcerer," I muttered. It was evil to touch myself thus. Only one who was evil could make me.

But he hadn't felt evil; he hadn't smelled evil. He definitely hadn't tasted evil.

What did evil taste like?

I splashed the now-cooling water over my flushed chest and neck. I'd allowed myself to be captivated once before, and look where that had gotten me.

Trapped in marriage to a man I loathed, one who was bent on getting me with child and—

I trembled at the thought. I'd watched my mother die in childbirth. I wanted no part of it. Not that what I wanted ever came into play.

Unless I was stalking a tibonage through the darkest hours of the night.

With my body yet tingling, I climbed out of the bath, wrapping myself in a robe, before snatching a hairbrush and moving onto the balcony, where a balmy breeze blew.

Once there, I untangled my hair, the air across the damp tresses and my moist flesh chilling me almost as much as the truth that governed my life.

Reginald had seduced me with pretty words and prettier promises. But once I'd believed his lies, nothing had been pretty anymore.

I doubted the dark stranger would be any different.

Chapter Six

"O! She doth teach the torches to burn bright."
—*Romeo and Juliet* (Act I, scene 5)

Will let the boy run off. He had no desire to seduce such innocence.

And he could seduce him, of that Will had no doubt. He'd tasted longing on the lad's lips, seen it too in those astonishing black eyes.

Will had kissed a man before, but never like this. The single time he'd tried, in need of something to make the endless nights less endless, he'd been unmoved. He was a woman's man, even though he was no longer truly a man.

The youth had only been gone a few moments when Will recalled that he still did not know how the boy had come to be a hunter, who had taught him, and why?

Will's speed was such that no human could outrun him, and now that he had the child's scent, so distinct, so exquisite, Will could follow him anywhere.

"Summer's breath," Will murmured. "Of sweet death are sweetest odors made." Oh, how he wished for paper and quill!

Though in legend Will's kind were depicted as becoming

heartless, murdering monsters upon their change, in reality, the only permanent change was physical.

To wit, if you were a heartless, murdering monster before, then you would be one still. And if you were a sensitive playwright whilst human, a sensitive playwright you would remain once undead.

Certainly there was a period where the awakening of bloodlust was like the youthful awakening of desire. At first out of control, never enough, always wanting more, but as time passes, it tempers. Creatures such as he became again who they once were, if who they once were was who they were still inclined to be.

Which was why Will's sudden yearning for a boy disturbed him. Such need he had never felt before in either lifetime. Would he soon long for human blood, a craving he'd believed long conquered? Would he once again feel compelled to raise zombies that would wreak havoc upon the presently peaceful isle Will had always called home?

Forsooth, he could have the lad's blood. Will possessed the ability to "push" humans, to make them act, then forget. He might take just a taste; the child would never know. All Will need do was lick the wound but once, and it would heal.

But Will would not. He'd worked too hard and suffered too long to go back to the way he had been when first changed.

Dying of some disease—mayhap the plague, who knew?—Will had been given a choice: Perish or embrace a new life. With stories swirling in his head that had never been put into words, still young with so much yet to do, Will had chosen this. However, the one who had made him that day, in a hovel, on a hill in the British countryside, had neglected to explain exactly what "this" entailed.

To be fair, the vampire that had changed Will had not known Will was a necromancer, that in addition to becoming a fiend with a taste for blood, Will would be able to raise the dead.

Will had never learned the man's name. He'd been so ill, so very close to dying, he'd barely registered the face. His maker had appeared years younger even than Will—cheeks not yet sprouting a beard, perhaps mere hours past childhood when he, himself, was changed. Yet in those eyes had swirled the knowledge of the ages. Will would not be surprised if the man had been born in a time so long forgotten as to be unnamed.

But Will had never learned the truth. For instead of teaching him how to exist as a creature of the darkness, Will's maker had given Will "the gift," and moved on, leaving Will to learn about his new un-life on his own.

The first night that Will had strolled past a cemetery beneath the light of a full moon, he'd been confused when the graves spewed out their dead.

It had taken time and practice, but eventually Will had understood what he had done and learned not to do it unless he meant to. A full moon, the conscious reaching for those that were gone, a little mind pull, and *voilà*! The dead would walk.

Will watched as the boy approached a large manor house. If that was his residence, it explained much about his speech and knowledge of French. As Will had thought, the child was at least the son of a wealthy merchant, at most the heir to nobility.

However, instead of opening the front door and walking in, the youth slipped around the side and entered through the garden gate. When Will attempted to follow, he found it locked.

He could break the door with one hand, but Will did not want to leave behind proof he had come. He'd long ago discovered, when in doubt, secrecy won out. Instead, he waited until a servant appeared, ready to begin the day long before the occupants of the house awoke.

"Sirrah," Will hailed. "Who lives here?"

"Mr. and Mrs. Dymond, your worship."

"Have they a son?"

"Not yet."

"Perhaps a nephew? Cousin?" The servant shook his head. "A visitor."

"No, sir. Mr. Dymond is off to the New World, and the mistress stays home most days with her nurse."

"Her *nurse*?" Will asked. Why on earth would a wife need a nurse? Perhaps she was simpleminded.

A shuttered look came over the servant's face. "I must go."

Will lifted one finger, met the man's eye, and murmured, "Not yet."

As if in thrall, because he was, the servant said, "Yes, sir."

Though Will much preferred information freely given, there were occasions he made use of one of the gifts that came with immortality. By peering into the eyes of a human, he could exert his will upon them.

"Why does Mrs. Dymond require a nurse?"

"Her husband resides in Virginia a good portion of the year," said the servant in a voice as dead as Will's body.

This was one reason Will disliked using his power to attain knowledge. Enthralled humans tended to answer only the question asked and nothing more.

"Why does Mr. Dymond's absence require a nurse for a grown woman?"

"He would not be made a cuckold."

"She is wanton?"

"No, sir!" The servant appeared offended. Considering the hypnotism, this was a surprising amount of emotion to be displayed. He must respect his mistress mightily.

"Then why the spy?"

"He is very jealous."

"But has no reason to be?"

"Not that I have seen." The servant frowned and pursed his lips. There was more.

"Tell me," Will ordered.

Words spilled from the man's mouth. "Mr. Dymond has a friend from school days who whispers to him of betrayal."

"And he believes this man?"

"He has no reason to mistrust. They have been friends for more years than he has been married."

The plot intrigued Will. He'd been alive long enough to know that the motivations for behavior were many and muddled. It was one reason he so enjoyed writing tragedies. Anything could happen for any reason and cause no end of trouble.

"You did not see me." Will stared deeply into the servant's eyes, imposing his superior resolve. "You remember naught of our conversation. Begone," he said, and looked away. He did not need to look back. The man would be gone. He would forget. He had no other choice.

Deep in thought over what the servant had revealed—a husband's jealousy, a friend's whispers of betrayal, a wife's innocence—Will remained standing on the far side of the garden wall.

The story made him think of one he'd read years ago in Italian—*Un Capitano Moro,* or *A Moorish Captain,* written by Cinthio. He had not remembered it until just now.

Will's fingers itched for his quill, and he turned away, the boy forgotten as a new play took shape in his mind. The Moorish captain with a lovely wife, his evil friend who whispers untruths and brings forth tragedy.

Suddenly a soft, sweet sigh drifted through the night, "Ay, me."

Will stilled. *That voice.* He could have sworn he'd heard it before.

He leaped over the wall and landed lightly within the garden. His gaze lifted, and he found himself entranced by the woman leaning her cheek upon her palm on the balcony.

"She speaks," he whispered as his skin prickled with a chill.

Her hair black and flowing free around her rose-hued face; her eyes, with lashes like a butterfly's wings, were as dark and as bright as the night sheen above. The robe white and thin, the shade of her skin beneath caused it to glow pale orange, like the hint of the lost sun at dawn. The slight curve of her breast and hip entranced him.

Will swallowed, thrilled as his body responded in the usual fashion to the sight of a beautiful woman.

"Speak again," he begged. "Oh, bright angel, speak again."

"My only love sprung from my only hate," she said. "Dark stranger, dark stranger, where are you tonight, dark stranger?"

That voice. That cheek. That chin.

Will suddenly understood why he'd been lusting after a zombie-hunting boy.

Chapter Seven

"Can one desire too much of a good thing?"

—*As You Like It* (Act IV, scene 1)

I had been speaking aloud as I was wont to do. Most times I spoke to Nounou, but then most times I spoke of zombies. Tonight the dark stranger filled my thoughts.

"Deny my father," I murmured. And my husband too. Ah, sweet denial.

A rustle from beneath made me catch my breath; then a man's voice nigh made me shriek.

"Shall I hear more," he said, "or shall I speak at this?"

I stepped back. "Who goes there?"

"I cannot tell you, for I am hateful to you."

Slowly I crept forward but saw nothing, no one, but still . . . I had not heard him speak a hundred words, yet I knew that voice. And if the dark stranger was here, he had followed me, which meant he knew my secret. Did he mean to tell Reginald?

My husband possessed an irrational jealousy. Strange, considering I'd never given him cause, and he cared not a whit for me at all.

A shout from the stables, another answering from nearer the house made me duck lower, speak softer. "How did you come to be here? The walls are high and hard to climb, and the place death if anyone should find you."

The man moved into the small sliver of light from the moon, and I could no more breathe than speak.

"With love's light wings did I o'er-perch these walls; for stony limits cannot hold love out."

He spoke so formally, yet beautifully, the words flowing like poetry. Reginald had once spoken to me thus.

At the memory, any excitement that had been within me at the sight of the stranger shriveled and died. I knew better than to be taken in by words, however pretty they might be.

"Love," I scoffed. "You are mad."

"Mad with love."

"You can't love me; you barely know me."

"I would know all if you but let me."

"No doubt," I muttered.

Nevertheless, my skin tingled. My face flushed. I wanted nothing more than to leap to the ground and let him kiss me and kiss me and kiss me.

I was a slut, and he was a sorcerer.

I had to make him leave. Preferably after I made him believe the boy he had kissed and the woman he had spied upon were not the same person.

I held my gown closed at my neck and stiffened as if outraged. "Sir! How dare you accost a woman outside her bedchamber? If I let out a single shout, you will be hauled to Newgate. Begone!"

He climbed the trellis, his movements so quick and agile

I did not have time to gasp or even move back before he was upon me.

"Fie!" I snapped, and held out my hand to halt him. "Come no farther. If they see you, they will murder you!"

"I have night's cloak to hide me from their sight."

He did blend into the shadows like smoke into the clouds. I had no more seen him in the garden than I'd seen him at first this night. However, hanging from the trellis on my balcony was another matter entirely.

"What is it that you will?" I asked.

"One kiss, and I'll descend."

"You think I would kiss a stranger who appears in my garden at night. You *are* mad."

"You kissed a stranger who appeared in an alley at night."

He knew.

I was not surprised. Yet still I must make him doubt.

"I am a gentlewoman, sir. You would no sooner find me in an alley than you'd find me . . ." My mind searched for an adequate comparison.

"Killing zombies?" His brow lifted, and his full, soft, delightfully cool lips quirked.

"Zombies," I mocked. "The more you speak, the madder you sound."

"You may deny it all you like, Dark Lady, but I have kissed you, and I would recognize you anywhere."

Panic began to flutter beneath my breasts like the wings of a poor trapped bird, and I blurted, "You kissed a boy, sirrah. I would not be touting that about if I were you."

His grin alerted me to my mistake. The only ones in that alley had been he and I. If there'd been a doubt in his mind as to my true identity, I had just ended it.

Fool!

"If you think I will pay for your silence, you need think again."

A scowl marred his smooth, sweet lips. "How could you believe such a thing?"

"How could I not? You kiss a boy, then you follow him home—"

"The scent of you enchanted me. Your eyes, that cheek. I could no more resist you than I could harm you."

I was not sure what was truth and what was lies. But that had forever been my problem.

"'Twas a sin to kiss me," I began.

Reaching out, he touched my cheek, his fingers like winter rain upon me. "Give me my sin again," he whispered.

His breath fresh and sweet, his lips so cool and soft, I could think of nothing but him. I leaned over the rail, my fingers in his hair. He strained upward, his hand still upon my cheek.

"Child?"

I tore away. Was the madness catching?

"Anon, good nurse," I called. My gaze still caught by his, I hurried inside before Nurse decided to come out.

She stared into the empty tub as if she might discover me within. When I grasped her shoulder, she shrieked. A thump and a curse from outside made me once again thankful for the woman's profound deafness.

"There ye are!" Nurse shouted.

I held up the hairbrush, then pointed to the balcony. "I answered your call."

"Time for bed," Nurse announced, as if she'd heard naught I said, which was no doubt the case.

I decided it was best if I complied and got rid of the

woman as quickly as possible. I allowed Nurse to pull up the covers, pat me on the head. 'Twas times like these I missed Nounou terribly. I had always felt safe with my own nurse, and her sword, so near.

No sooner had the door shut behind the old woman than I was up, across the floor, and slipping onto the balcony. I glanced over the edge.

No one was there.

My chest went tight, I knew not why. His being gone was for the best. I'd already decided I should never see him again. He was a weakness I could ill afford.

"Tell me, Dark Lady—"

I spun about. He was part of the shadows once more; I could only make out a wisp of his outline, a mere, slight sheen of his eyes. He could stand as still as death; he appeared barely breathing.

"How is it that you know of zombies?" he murmured.

I opened my mouth—to ask why he called me Dark Lady or to tell him the truth?—I never knew because before I could speak, I heard again, "Child?"

Would the woman never leave me alone?

"Anon!" I shouted, and the dark stranger started. At least I could see him better when he moved.

"Three words," I whispered, "and good night indeed. We must speak, so send me word tomorrow where and what time. Early morn perchance."

He stepped out of the darkness, into the moonlight, his face pained. "We must only meet at night."

"Madam!"

I let out a growl of exasperation, and called, "By and by I come!" then turned to the stranger. He was close enough to touch, and oh how I wanted to. Which was probably why my voice was sharp when I asked, "Why can you not meet in the morn? Are you married?"

"Are you?"

I remained silent. *Give me my sin again, indeed.*

"Send me word," I repeated. "Where to meet and when."

"Tomorrow eve," he murmured. "'Tis twenty years until then."

My dark stranger went over the rail in a nimble movement that nevertheless had me rushing forward, afraid he would fall. I peered over the edge, but he was already standing on the ground.

"How did you—?"

"Good night, good night!" he said just above a whisper. "Parting is such sweet sorrow, that I shall say good night till it be morrow."

Then he disappeared into the shadows.

"Wait!" I called. He reappeared. "What is your name?"

He smiled then, a wicked grin that when combined with the short, sharp beard and golden earring made me think of marauders on the high seas.

"William Shakespeare, Dark Lady." Bowing low, he glanced up whilst holding both the bow and the smile in place. "Anything you desire shall be yours."

Chapter Eight

"The game is up."
—*Cymbeline* (Act III, scene 3)

Will must have been mad to agree to meet his Dark Lady on the morrow. But he could no more say no to her than he could keep himself from touching her.

He was hearing the words again, the phrases that were like music. He could see characters; they'd begun to speak, and the plots, ah the plots, they were rolling through his head like honey.

And all because he'd kissed her.

The last time he'd felt like this about a woman, he'd lost her. First to Caesar, then to Antony, then to an asp. From the beginning, snakes had always been a problem.

Someday he would write about Cleo, but not yet. She still haunted him. Literally.

Or at least she had. Lately, Cleo had been as silent as Will's muse.

Although he'd wished often during the nights she'd appeared to him, talked to him, begged him to write her story that Cleo would go forever away, lately he'd begun to hope against hope that she would come back. Maybe now she would.

Britain before the Romans had been a very boring place, and when they'd come the first time in 55 B.C. Will had been a vampire for only a few years. He was running out of money, unable to do any sort of work since he was too newly made to walk in the light of day. He'd taken to raising zombies for sport; no one could afford a zombie army.

Until Caesar came into Will's life.

When the Romans had left, Will had gone along, and he'd raised his first zombie army for Caesar. If he'd been less captivated by Cleo, less brokenhearted when she'd left him for another, he might have raised one for her and thus changed the course of history.

Another reason he'd stopped creating armies. History was too much responsibility for any man.

Morning sped toward the horizon, and Will became lethargic as day pushed against the night. If he was still outside at first light, he would not be meeting his Dark Lady—what was her *name*?—this eve or any other.

The instant the sun burst over the hill, he would fall on his face like the dead man he was, and he would not move until the sun crept past its apex. If still outside, he wouldn't move *then* except as ashes blowing away upon a morning breeze.

Just like the zombies.

Will winced at the thought of what his Dark Lady would say if she saw that. She would curse him for a fiend; she would hate him forever.

He couldn't bear it. He must keep her from learning his truth.

'Twould be better for both of them if he never sent her word of where to meet, if he never went near her again. Of course, by telling her his name, he'd no doubt ruined any chance he had of avoiding her. Though her eyes shied away, and her words mocked him, her lips called to his. He'd lived a long time; he'd known many women, and he believed that if he did not meet with his Dark Lady, she would make it her mission to meet with him.

"As if you could live out eternity without ever seeing her again," Will muttered.

Not only had he been captivated by her face and voice when he'd believed her to be a boy, but her scent, her eyes, the brilliant bravery of her lionlike heart had brought words back to his parched soul. He could no more refuse to see her again than he could meet the sun in the morn.

Will nearly made it home. Would have, if he had not felt a telltale tickle, looked up, and caught a glimpse of that shambling corpse.

"God's blessing on my beard!" Will muttered. Why hadn't he borrowed his Dark Lady's sword? For that matter, why hadn't he brought his own?

The dilemma was neither here nor there. He had an adequate weapon in his hands. He must deal with the fiend before it escaped him. Heaven only knew what it was after.

Will followed the zombie into a part of London few dared tread, a dark section of Southwark, far away from the theaters and public houses, where desperate people lived desperate lives.

The houses were old and broken, the roads bumpy and poorly treated. Yesterday's rain still glistened in myriad dimples, the moon a rippling reflection atop those many pools.

Thieves, pickpockets, and whores, 'twas here they made their homes.

· No one accosted the fiend though many could have. The streets were fair crowded with thugs. Had the creature begun to smell?

Will lifted his face, took a tentative sniff, gagged.

Aye.

The just-risen are considered "dry," their flesh not yet moist enough to be offensive. The infusion of fresh brains keeps them that way. Without it, they begin to rot.

Fortunately, humans have speed and intelligence; zombies don't. Which makes it a bit difficult to gather enough brains to stay unpolluted, especially when there is an army's worth of zombies searching for nourishment. More often than not, some, if not all, of them begin to decay.

Which was why whenever Will had summoned a zombie army, he had done so as close to the eve of battle as possible. Not that a scented army was a bad thing. One that was large enough could cause a foe standing downwind to run instead of fight.

The problem lay in keeping such an army a secret. If the enemy knew a zombie force was coming, they could commission something worse.

Will had never been sure what "worse" might be, because he'd made certain to go about his business quietly and had therefore never run into such a problem. Of course *never* wasn't a word creatures like Will should even utter.

He frowned as the zombie ducked into a tattered home just ahead. Glancing into the hole in the thatch wall that served for a window, Will's eyes watered from the stench. There had to be a dozen of them in there, and they were . . . ripe.

"Amateur," Will muttered.

He could kill all the zombies within—Will searched his pocket for a tinderbox—and he would. But until he found the source, there'd only be more to come.

Will strolled around the building, which appeared far enough away from any others to avoid their catching on fire as well. He didn't want to set all of London ablaze. If Will touched a flame to each wall, top and bottom, then blocked the door—there was a large, abandoned carriage with a broken wheel nearby that would suit—his plan should work.

It would be difficult if not impossible to behead a dozen zombies on his own. But he *could* burn them to endless death—ashes were ashes after all.

Glancing around, Will was unsurprised to discover the area had become deserted. Those who prey on others quickly learn to recognize bigger and better predators.

Like him.

Will hoisted the carriage and transported it to the front door, careful not to let anything rattle and alert the creatures within. Then he made use of his flint to light one corner of the building down low. He snatched a piece of thatch, stuck it into the flames, then lit the corner of every wall and the adjoining roof area around the structure. The place caught fire like dry grass in August.

No doubt the zombies had been ordered inside before dawn and told not to leave. However, zombies are no longer human. They more resemble the beasts. They take orders better than any recruit in any army on earth, but if threatened they will do all that is in their power to survive.

Jumbled sounds rose along with the smoke.

"Aaaaye!"

"Erk!"

"Iglablud!"

The creatures tried to toss the carriage out of the way, but the door was too narrow. They all crowded in, jamming the doorway, then they couldn't get enough zombie hands through the opening to overturn the heavy, cumbersome vehicle.

"Perfect," Will whispered, his gaze on the steadily lightening sky. If he ran, he could make it home before he became ashes himself. Will took a few steps, and a dull creak shattered the night.

He expected to see the roof caving in, fire shooting up. Perhaps arms reaching skyward, legs kicking in death throes. At the least he should have seen ashes so thick they obscured the red-and-orange dance of the flames.

Instead, the near wall split, and zombies poured out.

Chapter Nine

"The common curse of mankind,—folly
and ignorance."

—*Troilus and Cressida* (Act II, scene 3)

"William Shakespeare," I whispered, staring at the shadowed portion of the garden where he'd disappeared.

I knew of him.

Who didn't in London these days? He was the most talked-about young man in the theater. A few months back a tirade by the late Robert Greene had been printed, which proved how jealous the old man had been of the "upstart Crow" who, "beautified with our feathers, . . . supposes he is well able to bombast out a blanke verse as the best of you."

Only for a great talent would Greene have bothered to write such an epistle.

I had yet to see Shakespeare on the stage, though I'd wanted to. Now, I wanted so much more than just to see him. I wanted things from Will Shakespeare I'd heretofore but imagined.

"God's ankles!" I muttered. "How can I dream such about a stranger?"

And a man. I had no use for men. The ones already in my life were trouble enough. What would I do with another?

Images tumbled through my mind of exactly what I would do with Will, and my skin flushed once more. The man's madness was contagious.

"I am a fool," I whispered. But I was a fool who would meet William Shakespeare again no matter the cost.

I awoke early to a day bright with memories after a night filled with dreams. Remembering them made me blush. Nothing good could come of these feelings, these dreams. I'd had them once before for a silver-tongued man, and what had happened when I'd given in to them had nigh ruined my life.

A brisk session with my rapier always made me feel more myself, and I needn't worry that Nurse would discover me thus and tattle to Reginald. He was aware of my fascination with sharp weapons of battle. Which was, perchance, why he treated me more gently than he treated anyone else.

My father was a master swordsman, and I had often watched him as he practiced. He was graceful with a sword. I had so wanted to be like him.

I'd begged and begged, made a proper nuisance of myself, until eventually he'd relented and taught me everything. Reginald had not been impressed or amused, but thus far he had not taken away my weapons or forbid me from continuing.

Whenever he was home, I made a point *not* to bring up the subject or take out my rapier. The less said, the less seen, the better. I often wondered what I would do if the plantation ever made a profit, and Reginald returned to England to stay.

Jump off London Bridge most like.

By the time Nurse invaded, my nightgown was as damp with sweat as my hair, and I felt as if I could take on a dozen zombies.

I knew better, of course. Only four at a time as Nounou had taught me. More and I was asking to be as dead as they. Zombies might be stupid, but they were still born to kill.

"Child! Child!" Nurse shouted, making me glad I was an early riser. If I'd been abed and awoken like that, my heart might not have withstood the shock. "You would not believe what has happened!"

I had just parried and thrust, but now froze, rapier out-stretched, opposing arm in the air for balance. Had Will been caught in the garden? Had he been arrested? Had he been hurt? Killed? Eaten?

The thought of Will's brilliant, beautiful brain in the belly of a walking corpse made me a bit faint, and I swayed.

"Madam!"

I jerked at the cry and smacked Nurse in the arse with my sword.

"Erp!" Nurse leaped a good foot in the air before coming back down with a solid *thump-thud*.

I clutched at her, afraid I'd truly injured the woman. "Are you hurt?"

Nurse clutched at me, staring into my face. "Are ye faint?" She laid her hand against my forehead. It came away damp, and her eyes widened. "Yer burnin' up, and yer face is bright red."

Since Nurse didn't appear to be bleeding, and hadn't bothered to answer my question, I assumed she was unharmed. I must be more careful in the future. Sticking zombies was one thing. Sticking humans quite another.

"Child!" Nurse thundered. "Are ye faint?"

"I was—" I meant to say that I'd been practicing, which always made me flush and sweat, but then I saw my way out. "Feeling a bit ill," I finished.

"Lord a mercy!" Nurse wrung her hands. "The babe."

If there had been a babe, the poor mite would be as deaf as Nurse before it was even birthed.

"I believe I will just lie abed today."

"Aye!" Nurse agreed eagerly. "Aye!"

I tossed off the damp gown, and when I held out my hand, a new one fell into it. Nurse might be annoying, but she was efficient.

"'Tis good that ye'll not be about. I'd come here to tell ye just that."

In the midst of climbing beneath the coverlet, I frowned. How could I have forgotten my fears about Will?

"Tell me *what*?" I demanded.

"That ye shouldn't be about," Nurse said even more loudly than usual.

"Yes, I *heard* you. But why?"

Nurse glanced around with a conspiratorial expression, then leaned over and roared in my ear, "The plague!"

A cold sweat sprang out on my brow, and I felt truly ill. "In London?"

Nurse nodded so adamantly her mainsail kerchief nearly slapped me in the face. "There are citizens wandering the night moaning; they have terrible sores. And some—" She took a breath that shook in the middle, her face reflecting her horror. "Their limbs be falling off. None have seen the like before."

I let out the breath I'd been holding. *Not* the plague, praise God.

"Others are bein' found with their heads burst open and their brains strewn about. Folks think the fever is makin' them explode."

I winced. Not fever. But zombies.

"In years past," Nurse continued as she moved around the room straightening my clothes and night table, "nearly thirty now—ye were not even born—the plague took nigh on eighty thousand people from England."

I had heard the story before, yet no matter how many times it was retold, I got a chill along the back of my neck. I hoped such horror would never happen again, but the hope was as empty as Reginald's heart.

"I lost my husband and mine own babe," Nurse said in a voice so quiet I barely heard. "My sister and her entire family, along with one brother and my elderly papa."

According to my father, a goodly portion of London's population had died during that particular epidemic.

The Queen had a very real fear of the plague. The instant she heard that a death in London could be attributed to the disease, she would hie herself to the country.

In 1563, she'd barricaded the court inside Windsor Castle, then erected a gallows and threatened to hang anyone who approached from London. I had to admire that. Of course, there was much about the Queen that I admired.

"Ye must stay within," Nurse continued. "Breathe ye not of the air." She slammed shut the balcony doors.

I was immediately engulfed in shadows. If I'd actually

thought I would be trapped inside until the Black Death played out, I would have gone mad.

"Yes, good nurse," I murmured obediently, and closed my eyes.

Nurse continued to stand by the bed and stare at me. I opened them once more. "I cannot sleep with you hovering."

"The master, he—"

I laid the back of my hand against my forehead. "Ah me, my head near threatens to split with your prattle. Would it not be terrible if the babe is lost due to my lack of rest?"

Nurse started as if I had poked her again in the backside, then she moved toward the door. "By and by, I'll come again and bring ye bread and ale."

I ground my teeth. "Nay. You wake me when you do. Stay out until I give you leave to enter. I am not hungry now."

Nurse blinked. "But—"

"Do as I say, Nurse, or I will not be responsible for what happens when my husband returns."

Nurse blinked several more times as my words wiggled into her thick skull. "As you wish, Madam." She bobbed a curtsy and disappeared.

If I'd known using Reginald's ire as a threat would work so well, I'd have begun doing so the day Nurse arrived.

I crept from the bed, and within minutes, I'd donned my clothes.

Will Shakespeare knew more than he was saying about the zombies, and with them overrunning London like the plague, I needed to know what it was.

I could not tarry through an endless day waiting for a message that might never come.

I would go to him at the Rose.

Chapter Ten

"The better part of valour is discretion."
—*Henry IV Part I* (Act V, scene 4)

The sight of over a dozen zombies shambling from the burning building, hair on fire, arms outstretched and mouths open wide, shrieking unintelligibly as they headed straight for him, turned any courage Will had possessed to a sudden and undeniable need to be anywhere but there.

So he ran.

Will could have outdistanced them. The ones on fire would eventually disintegrate, the ones that weren't would lose interest once the immediate danger to their existence, and hence their orders, had passed.

However, dawn threatened. He had to find a place where he could escape the morning light, and he had to find it now.

The sky had turned pink; a thin line of gold illuminated the horizon. The instant the sun burst past that line, Will would burst into ashes.

He ran down one street, then around the next corner, hoping to duck inside before the pack of zombies made the turn and saw where he had gone.

The area was still deserted, praise the saints, the fewer people who saw the pack of walking, flaming corpses the better. Ahead, he glimpsed a building that appeared empty. As he came closer he saw why. A white cross had been painted on the door.

"Plague," he muttered, then slipped inside.

Lethargy gripped him, but he managed to peek out the window as the herd of zombies shambled by, toenails clicking on the cobblestones like hail during a hailstorm. His ruse had worked. Not that it was very difficult to fool a zombie.

Will glanced around the cottage, and his eyes widened. Blood was splashed across the walls. Upon the floor, particles of brain matter had dried to a crust. Understanding dawned like the sun.

"Not the plague," he said to the empty room. "Zombies." Although weren't zombies just a movable plague?

Footsteps sounded outside—a lot of them. Will caught sight of the mob lurching in his direction.

"'Sblood," he whispered. They were back.

He must hide. In seconds he'd be on the floor sleeping the sleep of the undead. Then he'd wake up with a lot less brains than he'd fallen asleep with.

If he woke up at all.

Certainly it was damned difficult to kill him—many had tried—but it wasn't impossible. However, for all he knew, having his brains eaten by the risen dead might be a method as effective as decapitation. He didn't plan to find out.

Frantic, Will turned in a circle, looking for a place to disappear. Exhausted, he dragged his feet, shambling along as pathetically as a zombie himself.

The toe of his boot caught on a crack in the floor, and

down he went, barely managing to bring up his deadened arms and impede his fall before his face kissed wood.

When he landed, a loose board rattled, then turned over. Beneath it lay a hollowed-out section under the house. Will had just enough time to roll in and pull the board into place before the hellish fiends poured into the room.

How had they determined where he was? The zombies he'd known had never been very good at deduction.

They milled about; the thud of their feet echoed loudly all around him. "Br-br-br—" they began to chant, a dozen voices all raised in nonsense.

Will wished for perhaps the hundredth time that he was home. There was no place like it.

There's no place like home.

The words echoed in his mind, louder than the zombie's chant. Such sweet words and so true. He could build a story around them—perhaps a fanciful one. A storm, a girl, and her little dog too. Mayhap a witch. A colorful world unlike his own, where the child was dropped straight out of a whirlwind, and then—

A thump sounded, so close the earth around Will seemed to vibrate, and he held his breath. The words, the idea, the images went poof, and he suddenly felt cold, not just because his body now drifted toward the deathlike sleep that arrived with dawn, but because he feared he would be trapped beneath this floor, alone for all eternity.

Chapter Eleven

"Once more into the breach, dear friends, once more."

—Henry V (Act III, scene I)

"I must speak with Master Shakespeare, please."

I made my request to an extremely large man who smelled like the inside of an ale tankard and appeared as if he'd slept in the stained doublet and breeches, both of which strained at the seams from his bulk. At the moment, he seemed to be the only living being inside the Rose.

"He ain't here."

I blinked. The man's voice was higher than mine.

"Might you know where he is?"

He peered into my face. "Who are you?"

"I'm—" I bit my lip. Who was I? At the moment a nameless youth searching for Shakespeare. What *was* my name? I'd never had to give one. An introduction to the zombies being unnecessary.

"Are ye daft, boy? Do you not know yer own name?"

I peered at the ground and blurted, "Clay."

"Like dirt?"

"Clayton, but my mama calls me Clay since my papa's name is Clayton too."

Stop talking, Kate.

The more I lied, the more lies I had to remember, and I had enough on my mind.

"Fine. You're Clay, and you're wantin' Master Shakespeare. Why?"

"I'm a—a . . . friend of his. He asked me to meet him." He had, just not right now.

"Friend." He looked me up and down with a strange expression. "Uh-huh."

I lifted my chin. "I am. His friend." If you called someone you'd kissed beneath the stars a friend.

He smirked. "Well, ye can't be much of a friend if ye do not know that Master Shakespeare never comes to the theater in the morn." His big head shook. "Never." He turned and walked away.

Searching the place would be pointless and would only make me look the fool. The Rose was open on one side, revealing that all three levels were as empty as any theater in London at this time of day.

I began to walk home. I didn't want to wait until I heard from Will to see him; I didn't want to wait until afternoon to find him. But what I wanted was seldom what I got, and I was heartily sick of it.

Though I should have gone straight home before Nurse forgot her orders and came into my room, instead I did what I wanted and enjoyed the lack of restrictions that came with being a boy.

I wandered from here to there along with the populace.

I even went into the most dangerous area of Southwark. It was daylight, and I was a male with a sword and a dagger. No one would bother me.

The freedom was intoxicating.

Many of the buildings were deserted, with holes in the lath-and-plaster walls and empty spaces atop the thatched roofs. Upon several doors I saw a painted white cross—the sign of the plague.

Since Nurse had informed me of the symptoms of this new outbreak, and I knew it was no plague, I stepped inside each marked house. Some were just empty; others were empty *and* stained with blood and brains. How could anyone believe that the way the afflicted behaved was due to nothing more than a virulent form of disease? Of course what else *would* they believe? That zombies were invading our land?

As I approached another house, a low murmur drifted on the breeze. The closer I got, the more distinct that murmur became.

"Br-br-br."

I set my hand on my sword and crept to the window. Then I placed my back to the wall and considered what I'd observed.

Half a dozen zombies sitting in a semicircle on the floor as if trying to conjure something from the dirt, all the while chanting, "Br-br-br." I'd never seen anything like it.

Zombies said "Br—" when there was *br—* to be had. But as far as I could tell, the only *br—* in the house was what was left of theirs. And from the smell of the place, any *br—* in their heads was rotting.

Zombies don't eat rotten brains. If they did, they'd be

eating one another. And if they attacked one another for sustenance every time they came together, that would defeat the purpose of raising them.

No. Zombies required live, fresh brains from live, fresh bodies to remain . . . well, *alive* wasn't exactly the word, but it was the only one I had.

So what were these fiends waiting for inside an empty house?

Since they couldn't answer me, and I didn't really care, I drew my sword and waded into the fray.

As they sat on the ground, lined up one next to the other like an offering to Diana, Goddess of the Hunt, I lopped off the heads of four in a single stroke.

The other two became ashes as they scrambled to their feet. Another three came in from the rear. If I'd known they were there, I would never have begun. Nounou's rules were the reason I was still alive, and one of them was *Never fight more than four of the tibonage at one time.*

I'd already broken it by going after six, but I figured six zombies sitting were about the same as four zombies standing.

And a partridge in a pear tree.

The three stragglers met their fate as easily as the first six. One. Two. Three. They practically ran right into my sword.

I checked behind the house, even inside the privy, but no one hid there who might have caused the risen dead to chant their mindless chant.

I remembered the other houses I'd seen—empty but for the blood and the spatter of brains. Had the zombies begun to lie in wait for humans in their very own homes?

How unlike them.

Something strange was going on, something different from anything that had gone on previously. I'd encountered more zombies in the past two days than I'd encountered in the past two months.

If this continued, I was going to need help.

Chapter Twelve

"There are more things in heaven and earth . . ."
—*Hamlet* (Act I, scene 5)

Will awoke. He took a deep, calming breath, and words spilled into his mind like rain.

"This holy fire of love," he murmured. "A dateless lively heat, still to—"

To what?

Will closed his eyes, breathed in again, and caught the scent of—

"The rose." His eyes opened, and he frowned. Two different sonnets. He felt them hovering at the edge of his mind. One about—

"Diana and—" He bit his lip. "Cupid. Yes. Cupid laid by his brand and fell asleep. A maid of Dian's this advantage found."

His fingers ached for a quill so badly he had to breathe in and out to calm himself. Again he caught the scent of—

"The rose looks fair, but fairer we it deem for that sweet odor which doth in it live."

Will's hands fair clenched with need. He had so many words in his mind he could think of nothing else.

He sat up and rapped his head against something solid above him. A loose plank rattled. Then everything that had happened came flooding back, drowning the words. They floated away, perhaps never to return, and he groaned aloud before he could stop himself.

Where had those words come from? His sleep was death, and the dead do not dream. Yet he'd awoken to images so strong, he could think of nothing but how to make them come alive upon the page.

Shadows hovered all around, and Will understood that he'd slept very late. Those at the Rose would be waiting for him.

Most days he awoke as the sun tipped over its apex. At his advanced age, only the morning sun was death to him. He could go about in the afternoon if he remained out of its direct glare. One of the reasons he loved England so much . . . the days and days of misty, cool rain and cloudy, gray skies allowed him to roam.

Will must have been extremely tired to sleep so long. Being chased by a dozen zombies would exhaust any man— even one who was no longer a man.

Will nearly sat up again. *The zombies!* Were they still here? He didn't think so. They were stupid, but they weren't deaf, and he had not been at all quiet, muttering sonnets and smacking himself against the ceiling of his temporary home. If the risen dead remained, they'd be tearing up the floor by now.

Tentatively, Will peeked out. He got a faceful of ashes for his trouble.

Will shoved the plank to the side and climbed free. Then he glanced around the empty cottage.

Someone had been busy.

Considering the scent of roses that lingered, he knew who that someone was.

"She saved you."

Will started so violently he nearly fell back into the hole. He stared, wide-eyed, at the woman in the corner. Had she been there a moment ago?

Tall and regal, with skin as dark as the night sky, she wore a strange costume. Colorful bands of cloth were wrapped about her body and another about her head. Her eyes gleamed in the light of the rising moon, yet they were as dark as the ashes that still swirled across the floor.

"Madam." Will tilted his head. "May I help you?"

White teeth flashed in her midnight face. "'Tis I who will help you."

She had a strange accent, one he'd never encountered before, and considering the incredible length of his life, this was surprising. *French,* he thought, *but something else too.* Something he could not put a name to but that made her voice ebb and flow like the rhythm of the tide.

"In what way will you help me?" Will knew better than to mention the ashes all over the house—ashes that had once been zombies. He didn't mind being viewed as an eccentric genius, but he preferred not to be confined to Bedlam.

"You cannot fight dem alone."

A chill passed through him. "Fight whom?"

Her teeth shone again; she bent down and scooped up a handful of ashes, then opened her hand and let them fly away on the wind. "Who do you t'ink?"

Silence fell. She waited; so did Will. At last he could not stand the wait any longer. "Zombies," he blurted. "You saw them?"

"I always see dem."

"You are a chasseur?"

"*Oui.*"

"Do you know Mistress Dymond?"

"Kat'erine," the woman said. "Kate. Yes. I know her."

"Kate," Will murmured. "Plain Kate. Bonny Kate. Sometimes Kate the curst. But Kate, the prettiest Kate in Christendom." Where had that come from? He wasn't sure; he never was. Sometimes writing was a gift, other times a curse, but it was always fascinating.

He liked the name Kate. Perhaps he'd use it in a play. A woman unlike others of her day—stronger, smarter, she needs no man, wants none. Then she meets one determined to tame her. Yes, he—

The woman clapped her hands. *"Faites attention!"*

"Pardon me." Will bowed, though he gritted his teeth in frustration as his idea fluttered and died. "I have been rude."

"You cannot help it." She shrugged. "You hear voices. I understand."

Will blinked. How did she know?

He opened his mouth to ask, and she continued to speak. He'd already been rude enough; he dared not interrupt.

"Kate dispatched de tibonage." She frowned. "She is taking risks. Dere were too many for her to confront here."

"Yet she dispatched them."

The woman cast him a quick glance, and he had the urge to apologize again.

"De more she kills, de more she wants to kill." She spread her long-fingered, graceful hands. "It is de fate of a chasseur."

"Do you know who is raising them?" Will asked.

Her gaze sharpened. "Do you?"

Will shook his head. "To raise and control this many of the dead, a certain type of being is needed."

"Necromancer," she said, and the word whispered around the room like the wind.

"*Oui,*" he agreed, and she smiled.

"But not *just* a necromancer."

Will lifted his gaze to hers, and her eyes glowed like the stars.

"A necromancer who has died and been lifted again. He is undead. *Loogaroo,*" she said.

"I don't know that word." It wasn't French, but it was close.

"Vampire," she translated, her smile deepening. "Like you."

Then the woman turned and walked through the wall.

Chapter Thirteen

"Out, out, brief candle! Life's but a walking shadow,
a poor player that struts and frets his hour upon the
stage and then is heard no more: It is a tale told by
an idiot, full of sound and fury, signifying nothing."

—*Macbeth* (Act V, scene 5)

I approached the manor house sometime after midday. Servants bustled here and there. The garden was particularly full of them.

"God's tongue," I cursed. How would I get back in?

Perhaps I should just walk through the front door. It would be a lot less conspicuous than climbing the trellis to the balcony.

I kept my head tilted down and assumed a youthful swagger. I'd discovered that though my complexion and my eyes were too dark for fashion, they were memorable—my skin smooth and unlined, my eyes framed by sooty, long lashes. I could act like a boy, but if anyone took the time to *see,* I did not look like one.

As usual, nobody took the time. People believed what was on the surface unless forced to peer beneath.

However, I'd no sooner stepped into the foyer than I was ordered to "Gather the chamber pots, boy, and be quick about it!"

"Aye," I said, and ran up the steps as if I could not wait to clean up the swill.

I went directly to my room, planning to disappear within. If anyone asked about the missing servant, they would not ask *me*. Unfortunately, my plan went awry when I caught sight of Nurse pacing back and forth, back and forth in front of the door.

She wrung her hands. "Should I go in?" she muttered. "Should I wait until she calls? What if she died while I waited too long?"

Died? Why on earth would I—

Oh! The plague!

I tilted my head. I suddenly had a wonderful, terrible idea.

Nurse turned just then and saw me. "Here, boy. Come. Anon!" She waved her long, bony fingers, and her mainsail kerchief shimmered as if rippled by a north wind. "I trow, every servant in this place is slower than the arrival of Christmas."

"Yes, Nurse." I attempted to make my voice deeper; nevertheless, it came out sounding very much like my own.

She didn't notice.

"Who sent ye here and why?" she demanded.

"I am to gather the chamber pots." I started past her. "I'll just get the mistress's and be gone."

"No!" She grabbed my arm, and I saw my chance.

I pulled free, my expression shocked. "Ye are burnin' up, good nurse. On fire ye are!" I backed away. "Yer face is flamin'!"

Nurse slapped her palms to her emaciated cheeks. "I feel it not!"

"And why would ye," I said, continuing to inch ever backward. "Yer hands are as heated as the rest of ye."

She dropped her arms, stiffened her spine. "I am not ill. I am *never* ill."

"So says everyone who's ever been ill. Help!" I shouted. "Help!"

Nurse's mouth dropped open as footsteps sounded on the steps. "I will have yer hide." She advanced.

She would try, but if she managed to escape from the room in the stables where she would soon be thrown, she would be unable to find the boy who had gotten her thrown there.

I let her catch me, shake me, shriek at me—the better to make her seem out of her head. By the time the others reached us, she was beating me about my shoulders, and I was hiding my face.

"She is feverish, deluded!" I shouted. "Her skin is like fire. She must stop touching me! Oh, I do not want to die!"

If I did say so myself, I was convincing. I worked up a sorry bout of tears over my threatened life. The others pulled Nurse off me, then away down the stairs and out of the house. They left me sobbing in a heap on the floor.

As soon as I was alone, I disappeared into my room. Within moments, I came out again as Katherine Dymond, mistress of the house.

"Nurse?" I called. "Oh, where is my good nurse?"

If I smiled too widely and called too brightly, no one seemed to notice. They were too thrilled to tell me that my servant would most likely die.

Chapter Fourteen

"All the world's a stage, and the
men and women merely players."

—*As You Like It* (Act II, scene 7)

The woman had been a ghost.

Will's only excuse for not realizing it before she walked through the wall was that he hadn't seen or spoken to a ghost in so long he'd nearly forgotten the possibility existed.

However, her being one explained a lot.

How she had known he could hear voices, for instance. How she'd known what he was.

Strangely, the understanding that she'd been a specter calmed his fears. No one on this earth knew his secrets. No one could tell Kate the truth. He would not have to see the budding attraction in her eyes turn first to disgust, then to hate. Will did not know if he could bear that.

It had been centuries since he'd felt this way.

No, he must be honest. He'd *never* felt this way. Not in all the aeons he'd un-lived. The emotions that had shot through him when he'd kissed Kate had been unlike any he'd ever experienced before. What he'd felt for Cleo paled in comparison.

When he'd lost the Queen of the Nile, he'd agonized over her for decades. If he lost Kate, he wasn't sure he could go on.

He sounded like a besotted fool. As Kate had said, he barely knew her, how could he love her?

The streets were fair deserted, and for an instant Will wondered why. Then he saw the painted white crosses upon house after house, and he understood. The zombies had been at work.

The Rose was in an uproar. Players and workers milled about the open area in front of the stage and spilled across its painted floor.

Will was at first confused. Why would they be so upset over his late arrival? Certainly it didn't happen often, but it *did* happen.

Edmond lumbered over, eyes wide in his fat, florid face. "Master Shakespeare!" Agitation caused his voice to be even higher than usual. "The plague is about. They say the theaters will be closed to prevent its spread."

That Will could ill afford. Certainly he had funds put away—he'd lived too long not to—but to suddenly become flush when he was but a player would invite suspicion. Will had learned that the hard way in Dacia—now known as Transylvania. He hadn't behaved human enough and had barely escaped the country in front of a pike-carrying mob.

"When would this happen?" Will asked.

"I do not know, Master. I only tell you what I heard them say on the street."

Edmond had a habit of repeating what "they" said. "They" were forever saying something.

"The Queen has left for Windsor Castle," Edmond continued.

Will couldn't blame her. If Queen Elizabeth died of the plague, the country would be devastated. She had no husband, no heir, and she had not named one. Civil war would not be far behind.

"War," Will whispered. The perfect reason to raise zombies. Was that what this was all about?

"Sir?" Edmond's voice shook.

Will waved his hand. "Words, phrases, thoughts."

Since Will often talked to himself, to corners, the ceiling, empty rooms, Edmond merely nodded and moved on. "I do not know what we will do. I am so afraid."

"First you must calm yourself," Will said. Becoming hysterical did no one any good.

Edmond tried, but he was unable to stop wringing his great hands and repeating all he had heard that day. "They say there is an animal loose in the city. One that preys upon the weak in the night. Tears out their throats it does, then leaves them to die in the muck."

Damnation! Will had wondered if the one raising the zombies was an amateur; now he was certain. Only the newly risen had so little control over their appetites. Only they would leave the evidence behind for everyone to see.

"You should not get so upset, Edmond," Will soothed. "I'm sure whatever is afoot in the city will soon be set right."

"But the theater—"

"Until the theaters are closed," Will interrupted, "we have work to do." Work would keep Edmond's mind, as well as everyone else's, off their troubles. At least while they were here.

"The play is the thing," Will said. "Always."

His company had been milling around, waiting to see what Will would say, what he might do. Will had learned long ago that the only thing to be done in certain situations was to move on.

The performance was haphazard, his actors too concerned with the threat of plague to concentrate on their lines or their movements as they should. Will would have been more worried, except the audience was nearly nonexistent for the same reason. If he didn't want to go bankrupt and end up once again in a traveling show, Will needed to do something about the zombies.

And he'd forgotten to send word to Kate where to meet him and when. Will hoped she wouldn't hold the failure of his overtaxed brain against him.

He walked onto the stage for Act V, scene 3, of *Henry VI,* portraying Suffolk, an English lord who sought to influence the kingdom through his love for a princess. Will loved this play. Too bad they'd have to move on to another soon. People became bored, and so did his players.

"Be what thou wilt, thou art my prisoner," Will announced, looking out at the audience, or lack of one, instead of at the boy who played the princess. "O fairest beauty, do not fear nor fly! For I will touch thee but with reverent hands; I kiss these fingers for eternal peace, and lay them gently on thy tender side. Who art thou? Say, that I may honor thee."

"Margaret my name, and daughter to a king."

At the first word, Will's heart nearly failed. Would have, if his heart still beat. Kate stood in the place of Thaddeus Comstock, a lad of fourteen who possessed the voice of an angel.

Silence pulsed. Kate had finished her line and now waited, along with everyone else, for Will to continue.

"An earl I am, and Suffolk am I call'd. Be not offended, nature's miracle—" Will was able to say his lines, hit his marks, all the while attempting to figure out why in hell Kate was here and Thaddeus wasn't.

"The plague," Kate whispered as he came near. "The boy fled."

Zounds! If that continued, Will would have to close the Rose himself; he would not need to await the orders of the Queen.

Kate stared at him expectantly.

"Oh!" His line! What *was* it?

"A token?" Kate murmured, and his place within the play immediately came to him. How was it that she knew the lines so well?

"Words sweetly placed and modestly directed." He came close to her, closer than was proper. But near enough that Suffolk, and Will Shakespeare, could feel her warmth and catch the red-rose scent of her hair. "But, madam, I must trouble you again; no loving token to his majesty?"

Margaret—*Ach,* Will thought, *she is Kate, but she behaves so very much as Princess Margaret would*—stepped back with a stiffened spine and a tilted chin. "Yes, my good lord, a pure unspotted heart, never yet taint with love, I send the king."

As Suffolk would and most likely did, Will followed Margaret—*Kate*—step by step across the stage, at last snaking his arm around her. "And this withal," he said, then kissed her.

And suddenly it was not Suffolk and Margaret on that stage but Will and Kate, Will and Kate, ah, Will and sweet Kate.

She tasted like warm, red wine in the middle of a long December night. He took her mouth, deeper and deeper still he delved, learning, laving, tasting.

Her breath intoxicating, her skin so soft. The flutter of her eyelashes cast a springtime breeze across his cheeks.

She clung to him, her fingers digging deep into the coarse wool doublet across his shoulders. Her response drew an answering one in him. Heat such as he hadn't known since he'd died pulsed in the winter of his blood.

Her breasts pressed against his chest, so round, so tempting. His palm slid from her waist ever upward, and out in the audience someone coughed.

Will let her go as if she were a pot that had suddenly boiled over. No wonder people thought he was a sodomite. A kiss like that with a boy—

Marry! He would never live it down.

"Line!" someone whispered from the wings.

Was the line his, or was it hers? He had no idea. Thankfully, Kate was not so witless.

"Th-that for thyself: I will not so presume, to send such peevish tokens to a king."

And with that she flounced out on the arm of Marcus Abbott, who played her father, Reignier. Will hadn't even noticed him on the stage, though he'd exchanged lines with the man when he'd arrived not five minutes past.

Who had thought it a good idea to put a woman in the place of a boy? The Rose could be shut down for such effrontery!

Nay, no one would have known Kate as a boy. Only Will did, and he must keep her secret. Even if it meant labeling himself a lover of men.

It wouldn't be the first time.

Chapter Fifteen

"Misery acquaints a man with strange bedfellows."
—*The Tempest* (Act II, scene 2)

My heart was beating far too fast from the excitement of actually stepping upon the stage at last. Combined with that kiss . . . I thought I might faint.

Except I did not faint. *Ever.* I was a chasseur and had much better things to do with my time.

Nevertheless, I was grateful for Mister Abbott's arm. I hoped he still believed me a boy pretending to be Margaret, the future Queen of England, and not a woman pretending to be a boy pretending to be a woman.

"Ah, me," I sighed. What a tangle.

I reached the wings, and Abbott dropped my arm as though I had the plague. I cast a quick glance in his direction and caught the curl of his lip.

That kiss. It was going to cause problems in more ways than one.

I lifted my chin. "I am an actor, sirrah," I said in my haughtiest young man's voice.

"You're a lot of things I'll trow," he said, and walked away.

I stared after him, surprised. Those who worked in the theater should be used to men who enjoyed men—for friendship, for companionship, for any "ship" that might pass in the night. It wasn't as if Will hadn't kissed the boy who'd portrayed Margaret just yesterday.

Fury flashed at the thought. If Thaddeus had been in front of me in that instant, I might have slapped him. How dare he kiss those lips that had kissed mine?

I rubbed my face as I shook my head. I wasn't certain, but I thought the irrational anger just might be jealousy. I'd never felt anything like the burning inner flare before, and I didn't much like it.

I put aside the strange emotion. I had to finish the play, and being distracted would not help me remember my lines. As it was, I frantically studied the next scene from the wings, thanking my maker for the gift of an incredible memory.

When the play ended and we'd taken our bows, I left the stage, but I turned back for one last look, and my nose slammed into Will's chest. How had he come upon me so suddenly and so quietly?

"Come with me." He took my arm and practically dragged me away.

"Sir!" My voice was too high; I sounded like a wronged woman. Will cast me a quick, dark glance, and I subsided.

At least until he pulled me into his room and kicked shut the door. I opened my mouth to berate him, and he backed me against the closed portal, then kissed me again.

I could have fought, and I would have won. I was not so foolish as to prance around a theater of men with nothing more to protect myself than their belief that I was a boy. As was evident right now, my being believed a boy meant naught to Master Shakespeare.

My dagger pressed against my calf. I had no doubt I could disable Will and grab my weapon. He might be all muscle beneath his doublet, but he wasn't a chasseur. He hadn't been fighting zombies for a good portion of his life.

I should stop him, stop this, but I couldn't. My body had been humming ever since Suffolk's lips had first graced Margaret's. The hum had become a throb in the next instant when the kiss became ours.

Kissing Will in full view of the audience, pathetic as their numbers had been, had, strangely, made the embrace more intimate. I'd felt as if we'd been doing the forbidden right there on the stage. At the least, I'd been *thinking* of it. From the way he was kissing me now and the hard, heated press of him, Will had had the same thoughts.

Loud voices beyond the door made me start and turn my face away. Will responded by kissing my cheek, my chin, my eyelid, my neck. I tangled my fingers in his hair. Ah, that felt heavenly.

"Clayton! Clay! Where is that boy?"

Low murmurs, a snicker, then footsteps. When I opened my eyes, Will stared into them.

"You should let me go," I said.

"Never."

"They will think we are—"

He brushed a stray hair from my face, the glide of skin against skin a caress. "They already do."

I tilted my head. "Does that bother you?"

"Does it bother you?"

"No."

He grinned and lowered his head to kiss me again. I put my palm to his chest. He immediately stopped, which meant more to me than the kiss itself.

"You do know that the punishment for such behavior is death?" I asked.

"I'd gladly die for one night in your arms."

I stiffened. Reginald had once said the same thing. Now he just wanted me to die in childbed.

The mood was ruined. Thinking of one's husband while in the arms of another man tended to do that. Or so I'd heard.

I slid from Will's embrace, and he let me, though his confusion at my sudden shift was evident.

"Kate." He attempted to snatch my hand, but I shoved them both behind my back. "You know that no one has been put to death for such things in years."

"Of course," I said absently, then— "How do you know my name?" I'd certainly never told him.

A shadow passed over his face, and he looked away. "I asked one of your servants."

A secret there I'd vow, but since I had secrets of my own, I let it pass. There were other questions I'd much rather hear the answers to. For instance . . .

"How is it that you know of zombies?"

"They're everywhere." Will glanced over his shoulder. "Lately."

"And why is that?"

"Do you know what type of creature raises a zombie?"

"Of course."

"Of course," he muttered, and glanced down, shoulders slumped.

"My nounou, my nurse, the one who taught me of the

tibonage, told me what kind of horrible hell-fiend brings them to life."

"Hell-fiend," Will repeated, and let out a short, sharp laugh that did not sound at all amused.

"Why do you repeat everything I say?"

"Why indeed?"

My teeth ground together. If he didn't stop that, I just might strangle him.

"What type of hell-fiend did your nurse believe raised zombies?"

"The undead. She called them loogaroo." I gave the word the foreign twist Nounou had always used.

"Vampire," Will whispered.

"How do you *know* all this?"

"I—" He took a breath, let it out slowly. "When you live the way I do, you see many things."

"Most people who encounter zombies refuse to believe what their eyes plainly see."

"I'm a writer. I live to imagine. I question. I search. I observe. I've traveled, not just in this country but others."

"And you've seen more than zombies," I said. "You've seen vampires."

His dark gaze flicked to mine, then away. "Yes."

"What are they like?"

"You and me." He shrugged. "You can't tell a vampire from a human."

"But"—I frowned—"do they not burn in the sunlight?"

"If they're stupid enough to walk into it. Most aren't."

"Won't a crucifix kill them?"

"Vampires predate Christ, Kate." His lips twisted. "A crucifix would not even slow one down."

"Garlic?"

"Horrific breath."

"Stake through the heart?"

"As their hearts no longer beat, putting a stake through it would do no harm at all." He took a deep breath. "No, to kill a vampire you must cleave the head from the body, same as a zombie."

"Truly?"

He shrugged and looked away. "So I've been told."

"All right," I said. "I can do that."

Will's gaze met mine once more, intense, concerned. "Best to do that when they're sleeping the sleep of the dead. Vampires are faster than the flicker of a flame, Kate, and stronger than can be believed. The only being that can truly fight a vampire is a vampire."

"But—"

"If you try, you'll discover your sword turned against you. Vampires are not something you want to anger. Like any beings—human or inhuman—they'll fight to live."

"But they aren't alive."

"They aren't dead either." He took a deep breath, then let it out slowly. "Not really."

"How do you know so much?" I repeated.

"I—" He bit his lip, then blurted, "I met a hunter once before."

There was more to it than he was saying. But again, I didn't press.

"Why do vampires raise zombies?" I wondered.

"Didn't your nurse explain?"

Nounou had died before she'd told me everything. Sometimes my lack of understanding worried me.

"She said they were evil, so raising evil minions was their calling." Will laughed, which made me frown. "It isn't?"

"Not all vampires raise zombies."

"I thought they couldn't help themselves."

His beautiful lips curved, making me remember his kiss, the way he'd tasted, the way he'd touched. Heat flared. I had to close my eyes for a moment and count to ten.

"Raising the dead requires skill and knowledge," Will said. "It can only be done by a certain class of undead: very rare, but powerful enough to raise an army. Literally."

My eyes widened as a chill came over me. "What makes them special?"

"In life, they had an affinity for the dead. They saw ghosts, spoke to them. They are called necromancers. When they become vampires, their power is magnified."

"God's toenails," I muttered. "A necri— Nacri— Necry—"

"Necro," Will said.

"A necro-vampire."

"'Tis as good a name as any," Will agreed.

"You think one of them is in London now?"

"At least one," he said, fixing his gaze on the closed door.

"What shall we do?"

He glanced at me, brow furrowed. "We?"

I didn't trust him with my body or my heart, but with a sword . . . maybe.

I wasn't stupid. I needed help. At least I wouldn't have to explain zombies, or vampires, to Will Shakespeare.

I reached for the rapier in the corner and tossed it in his direction. Will caught the weapon with one hand.

"How well do you handle a sword?" I asked.

Chapter Sixteen

"He does it with better grace, but I do it more natural."

—*Twelfth Night* (Act II, scene 3)

"Better than I should," Will answered.

"How so?" Kate reached down and whipped Margaret's dress over her head.

Will's mouth went as dry. He caught his breath, then immediately released it when her boy's clothes were revealed. Marry, she had not been disrobing, merely removing her costume. He must get his mind out of the chamber pot.

Kate tilted her head, awaiting his answer.

"Most—" His voice came out hoarse, and he coughed, swallowed, then tried again. "Most playwrights wield a quill better than a sword."

She leaned over and took up a second sword, then motioned him forward with a practiced flick of her slim wrist. "And you?"

She feinted; he parried. Steel clanged against steel. She withdrew, twirled, and this time she really tried to kill him.

Will barely managed to get his weapon up before she ran him through. She'd have been very upset when he didn't die.

Clang. Clang. Clang. CLANG! She came at him again.

"Umph," he said as Kate shoved him away, and he let her.

"Try!" she cried, so he did. Just a little.

He drove her back by sheer force, then became distracted by the slick slide of perspiration along her brow. She dropped to the floor, swept out with one foot, and knocked him off his. He hit the ground like a bundle of wood. She landed on his chest and drove the air right out of his lungs.

Not that he needed any.

The door opened. Both Will and Kate turned to look. Edmond and several of the stage crew stood in the hallway, eyes wide, mouths open. "We thought ye might need help, sir."

"Not since I was twelve," Will said. "Get out."

The door shut. Kate looked at Will; Will looked at Kate, and together they laughed.

"You're quite good for a man who makes his living in the theater." Kate climbed off him. He wanted very much to pull her back.

"Well"—he got up—"we do practice swordplay on the stage."

She laughed again, and the sound of her joy, the pure happiness on her face captivated him. While he was studying her, thinking of how he'd describe her laugh, her face in a sonnet—

"Sweets with sweets war not, joy delights in joy," he murmured.

She nearly ran him through.

"Pay attention!" she admonished. "If zombies had a brain, you'd be without yours."

Kate performed another fancy twist and slapped Will across the buttocks with the flat of her sword. By the time he caught up, the unprotected tip lay against his throat, just above the cloth he'd taken to wearing over the thin, red line, which was all that remained from his "death" in the alley. Without human blood, that mark could take weeks to heal.

"Lucky for you," she murmured, "the tibonage do not use a sword very well at all."

"Lucky." He swallowed, and the sharp end slid along his neck like a razor.

"Oh no!" Kate lifted the weapon. "I cut you."

Before he could stop her, Kate reached out, and when she drew back, a droplet of blood quivered on her skin. Ruby red and sienna, the colors of night. Would she put her lips to that blood? Might he?

Will's teeth flamed. He had to think of something else before his fangs sprang free.

"*En garde!*" he shouted, and lifted his sword. Shocked, Kate lifted hers, and they began to fight as if they meant it. It was the only way Will could think of to drive back his beast.

The idea worked. Kate was the best swordswoman he'd ever encountered. Forsooth, he hadn't encountered any. Women did not fight with swords. But, then, Kate wasn't just any woman.

"Who taught you?" he asked, his breath coming hard and fast as they circled the small room. He must keep up appearances. Perhaps he should trip once or twice.

"My father," she said. "He was a master and I his only child."

Most fathers would still refuse. Be she his only child or not.

"I must meet your father," he said.

"No." She came at him, her skill driving him back to the wall. "You must not."

Will's shoulders met the wood with a thud, and he found himself again with a sword to his throat. "Fine. I must not."

He was, after all, a mere playwright and she the daughter of a wealthy man. She'd been educated. She carried herself like a queen. Will was not of her class, and he never could be.

Kate dropped her weapon. "It isn't that I do not want you to meet him. But how would I explain . . ." She shrugged. "This?"

Will saw her point.

Married women didn't have male friends. Women did not go out at night to fight zombies. They did not act upon the stage.

"Your husband," he began.

"You will not speak of him."

Since she'd brought the rapier up, and it now hovered inches from his face, Will froze. He had not wanted to speak of him anyway.

Did she love the man? How could she and kiss Will the way that she had?

Kate dropped the weapon once more and turned away. Her shoulders slumped. Will would have given ten years of his un-life to hear her laugh again.

"Will you help me?" she asked. "I do not think I can fight them by myself any longer."

She couldn't. Will knew that better than anyone. So even for the sake of his own heart, which he was certain she would break, he couldn't leave her out there all alone.

"Yes." Will gently took the sword from her hand, his fingers lingering just a bit along the swell of her thumb. "I'll help you."

She didn't thank him. She merely nodded and opened the door. "I'll see you tomorrow," she said.

"We will hunt?"

"Perhaps after."

All sorts of images went through his mind about what "before" might be. He doubted any of them would come true. But one had to have hope.

Will opened his mouth, shut it again, swallowed, then repeated, "After?"

"Mr. Alleyn hired me to replace Thaddeus."

Edward Alleyn owned the Rose. Sometimes he acted; sometimes he directed too. But he provided a good portion of the money, and what he said was what happened.

Having Kate around during all Will's waking hours would only lead to disaster. Nevertheless, his soon-to-be-broken heart fluttered. He could have sworn it almost began to beat again.

Chapter Seventeen

"This grief is crowned with consolation."
—*Antony and Cleopatra* (Act I, scene 2)

"What time should I arrive?" I asked. Mr. Alleyn had only told me to do so.

Will didn't answer at first, just stood very still as though deep in thought.

"Will?" I murmured. I shouldn't be calling him by his given name. Then again, I'd sucked on his tongue. Should I really be calling him Master Shakespeare?

"Three o'clock," he said absently. He'd already gone away in his head to that place where he combined the perfect words into beautiful phrases that became the brilliant plays of a master.

I left him in his room, staring vacantly into space. If I'd come upon him like that anywhere else, I might have chopped off his head. When he was in the throes of creation, he behaved more like a zombie than a zombie.

I hurried home, climbed the trellis, listened for a moment, but with Nurse confined to the stable, my room was deserted.

Heaven had come to the earth.

I'd left orders that I alone would tend the woman. "She has taken care of me as no one else has," I'd said. "I can do nothing but the same."

A few of the older servants had tried to argue that I should not go near her, but when I'd insisted, they'd given in. No one wanted to care for a plague victim. They'd rather face Reginald's eventual wrath at the loss of his breeding stock than lose their lives themselves. And I could hardly blame them.

Inside my room, I quickly changed into an old gown, then made my way downstairs and across the short distance to the stables. The house, the outbuildings, and the garden felt deserted. Probably because the chill of the air and the cool, silver sheen of the moon made me lonely. I'm not sure why.

I stepped into the warm, golden glow of the stables. No one greeted me.

"Odd," I murmured. There should be a groom available at all hours. What if I'd needed a horse?

What I'd do with a horse since I'd never learned to ride I had no idea, but the fact remained that I should always be able to get one if I felt a sudden urge.

"Hello?" I called.

A small boy, hair as pale as flax, peeked from an empty stall, then immediately ducked back in.

"You can come out, child."

His white circle of a face appeared, then disappeared again. His high, shaky voice came from the depths of the darkness. "Be ye goin' to open the door of that room?"

"Yes. I must take care of my nurse."

"She has the plague they say."

"She does." For an instant, guilt flared as I lied to a child.

"It travels on the air. Ye open the door, and we'll all die."

He might be right. Except Nurse didn't have the plague. However, I couldn't tell him, or anyone else, that.

"I can't just leave her there," I said.

His short, sweet stub of a nose appeared. "She might be dead already."

A thud sounded from the other side of the door.

The nose quickly went back in. "Or not."

"You may run along," I called. "You need not stay. Take any others who fear the plague along with you."

"I'm all there is, Mistress."

I'd started toward the room that housed Nurse, who was now banging handily against the portal and shouting to be let out. But at his words, I turned back. His little face quickly disappeared into the gloom again. "All?" I murmured.

"They were afeared of dyin'."

"And so?"

"They ran off." He stepped from the stall and drew himself up to his tiny height. "'Cept me."

"Well, you *are* brave," I said. "What is your name?"

"Jamie. I'm an orphan."

Poor lamb.

"No one left in the house but Cook," he said.

That was fortunate, since I couldn't.

The boy glanced again at the door that had begun to shake with the force of Nurse's fury. "She sure is actin' outta her head even though she keeps shoutin' that she ain't sick."

"It is the way of the plague," I said. "They become like animals. I've seen them snarl and scratch and bite. Foam comes from their mouths, and their eyes—" Jamie's own, bright blue eyes had widened at my description. "Best if you run along now."

Jamie didn't have to be told twice. He ran. I wondered if he'd ever come back.

My plan was working out so much better than I could ever have hoped. Not only was Nurse locked up and out of my way, but the majority of the servants had left—no one to stop me from doing whatever I wanted to. I felt so free I thought I might fly.

Then I opened the door to Nurse's prison, and she barreled into me, knocking me completely off my feet. She would have made good her escape if I hadn't snatched her by the ankle as she ran by. I tugged, and she fell flat on her face with a shriek followed by an "oomph." All the air came out of her lungs in a whoosh, and her mouth opened and closed like a fish upon the shore.

I got to my feet and started to drag her back into the room. She recovered quicker than I would have thought possible and began to thrash.

One of her heels caught me in the eye, and I saw stars. How was it that a half-deaf old woman could knock me nigh onto senseless and half a dozen zombies couldn't?

"Need my sword," I muttered, concerned when my voice came out slurred.

"Duck," someone shouted, so I did.

Thunk!

Nurse fell like a downed tree. I turned my head. Jamie held a slice of wood the size of a sapling. How the boy had wielded it was as much a mystery as how he'd lifted it in the first place.

His shaggy hair shifted over his face as he picked up a good-sized stone that had rolled out of Nurse's hand. "She was gonna hit you."

He sounded as shocked as I felt. I'd never seen a hint of violence in the woman. Maybe she *did* have the plague.

"Thank you, Jamie." I sat a moment until my mind cleared, then took Nurse by both feet and dragged her into her room.

I no longer felt bad about leaving her there.

Chapter Eighteen

"The course of true love never did run smooth."
—*A Midsummer Night's Dream* (Act I, scene 1)

Will spent the rest of the night writing until his hand fair ached. It seemed that every time Kate came near, he couldn't find a quill fast enough.

He managed to compose a message to her before the dawn sent him into his deathlike sleep, informing her that plans had changed, and she should arrive at the Rose by half past twelve of the afternoon.

He needed to say these lines, walk the stage, figure out just what it was that he'd imagined all night long, and he wanted Kate with him to do it.

When Will awoke, his messenger had returned and gave him the news that Kate would be there anon.

At the stroke of 12:30 came a knock upon the door of the Rose. Will had ordered everyone out. Since he often did so when working on something new—there were idea thieves everywhere—no one thought his behavior strange.

However, if they'd seen Kate slip in, they would have. Since he'd had the beginnings of a play stolen out from under him and sold to an aspiring playwright by an unscrupulous crew member, Will worked alone.

Or maybe no one would have thought anything but that he couldn't get enough of her. Make that *him,* since Kate must needs arrive in the guise of the boy Clayton.

"I barely slept," she said. "My excitement for tonight was so great."

"You hunt night after night. I would think that much more exciting than this."

Will held his breath, waiting for her to say her excitement was because of him. If he'd been able to truly sleep, he doubted he would have either because of her.

Kate left a trail of sweetness in her wake as she moved toward the stage. "You do not understand what it is like to be told—nay, to *know*—that something you desire is forever beyond your reach."

He followed as though entranced. "Tell me more."

She stood with one boot upon the first step and another yet on the ground. "Since I was old enough to walk and to talk, I would pretend. I was King Hal, Queen Kate." She let out a light laugh. "One, two, or three—Aragon, Howard, or Parr—it mattered not. Then I was Princess Mary or Bess. Eventually I was the Queen."

"You are a queen," he murmured, and she shot him a quick glance over her shoulder.

It was then that he saw the bruise.

He was across the distance that separated them in an instant. Too fast, he thought, but she'd turned away; she hadn't seen, and he could cover ground so silently she didn't know he was there at all.

Until he touched her.

"Who hurt you?" he asked, and though his voice was soft, the growl beneath was anything but.

She turned, and his hand slid from her shoulder as her eyes widened, and she lifted her fingers to her blackened eye. "Oh," she whispered. "I'd forgotten."

He couldn't help it; he brushed his fingertips across the bruised skin. Instead of wincing, she sighed, as if his touch could heal.

Oh, how he wished that it could.

"I will kill him," he said.

"Him who?"

Then he remembered. Her husband was across the sea. Unless he'd come home.

"Who hit you?" Will demanded.

"'Twas an accident. A foot, my eye." She spread her hands and shrugged.

"Someone *kicked* you?" he thundered, and his teeth began to itch.

Her gaze had been so focused upon the stage and her dream of stepping onto it that she obviously hadn't noticed his increasing fury. Now she couldn't help it.

"Calm yourself," she said briskly, as if speaking to a child.

The tone worked; his teeth stopped itching.

"My nurse has lost her mind. It was necessary to confine her. She didn't go easily."

"Lost her mind," Will repeated. "Truly?"

"No." Kate took the few steps up to the stage and moved

to the center, gaze focused on the nonexistent crowd. "What is it like, Will, to be up here and be someone else? To hear the applause, to feel the . . ." She took a deep breath, and her eyes met his.

"Magic," he murmured.

"Yes."

He joined her. He'd get to the bottom of the black eye and crazy nurse in a moment. But for now he'd indulge sweet Kate. Forever would he like to indulge her.

"You want to know what it is like?"

She nodded.

"I'll show you."

He pulled the papers from inside his doublet, the ones he'd been working on all night, the ones that held the lines he wanted to say with her.

Will offered some; she took them from him. "A new play?"

"I'm not sure. Can we—? Would you—?"

"Read with you?" Her smile bloomed as bright as the stars. "I'd like nothing more."

They faced each other, and he began. "Even as the sun with purple-color'd face had ta'en his last leave of the weep-ing morn."

Kate read her lines from the page as if she'd read them a hundred times before. "If thou wilt deign this favor, for thy meed a thousand honey secrets shalt thou know: Here come and sit"—she spread her graceful hand to indicate an imaginary stool—"where never serpent hisses, and being set, I'll smother thee"—she lifted her gaze to his—"with kisses."

Will's throat went dry. He had to swallow twice before he could continue. "Ten kisses short as one, one long as twenty:

A summer's day will seem an hour but short, being wasted in such time-beguiling sport."

"Touch but my lips with those fair lips of thine."

Will didn't know when he'd moved closer, but he had, and now they stood hip to hip, chest to chest, her face tilted up, shaded by her cap, yet he could still see the full, ripe beauty of her. "Though mine be not so fair, yet are they red. The kiss shall be thine own as well as mine."

He leaned in and brushed his lips against hers. Her breath caught; so did his. Just that slight touch he felt everywhere.

Kate's face flooded with heat, and she glanced down, the brim of her cap scraping his nose. Will stepped back, then stretched out a hand to cup her chin. "What seest thou in the ground?" He lifted her exquisite face. "Hold up thy head: Look in mine eye balls, there thy beauty lies; then why not lips on lips since eyes on eyes?"

"Why not indeed?" she whispered, and kissed him.

Will forgot his next line; he could no longer remember hers. The paper slid to the floor as he cupped her face.

Ah, but soft.

She went onto her toes and pressed herself against him— her lips, her tongue, her chest—she wore too many clothes. Her skin so smooth, he wanted to touch every last inch of it.

Suddenly she pulled away—from his mouth, his hands. Her fingers rose, and she touched her lips, her eyes wide and a little scared.

He'd knocked her cap from her head. He had no recollection of that. Her hair, pinned tightly, had begun to tumble down. She appeared as if she'd been loved and well. He reached for her, and she stepped back. Words gushed into his head like water through a sluice.

"Beauty within itself should not be wasted. Fair flowers that are not gather'd in their prime rot and consume themselves in little time."

Her hand fell away. "Rhyming," she said. "A poem perhaps."

"What?" Will shook his head, which was full of more rhyming words. "Even so she kissed his brow, his cheek, his chin, and where she ends she doth anew begin."

Kate smiled and stepped closer. Then she kissed his brow, trailing her lips to his cheek and chin before leaning back, staring into his eyes. "Like that?" she whispered, and he was lost.

His mind blanked; every last word began to fade. His hands twitched; he should write them down before they disappeared forever. Which happened at times, and it was usually the very best of his words that vanished away.

But he didn't dare go searching for a quill and paper. Forsooth, he didn't care. Kate was here, and if her kiss was any indication, she was his.

He dived, filling his mouth with her taste, his hands with her skin. Or at least he wanted to. His palms traced her shoulders, her arms, her hips and swept upward. Her breasts were bound. He felt nothing but cloth.

The growl that rumbled in his chest should have frightened her. Would have if she were a normal woman. But Kate was a chasseur. She'd faced worse things than an aroused man. Instead of gasping in fright, she laughed.

He drank her mirth like the finest Madeira, licked the lightness from her lips like *licoresse.* When she stepped away, he followed, entranced. But she put her hand to his chest, and he froze.

"Are we alone?" she murmured. He could manage nothing beyond a nod. "For how long?"

Will found he could not speak, even to save his soul—could his soul be saved?—so he spread his hands.

Kate tilted her head, glanced below his waist, and her lips curved. "Long enough, I trow."

Then, praise every saint ever born, she began to unlace her doublet.

First the smooth line of her throat appeared, her skin the shade of the earth in August, when the blessed beat of the sun baked every last drop of moisture away. Will loved that shade. It brought to mind his days as a child, when he could play in the bright light of the day and never catch fire.

He would lick that skin; he would let the heat of her wash over him, then bask in that heat like a cat in the morning rays of the sun.

Kate's fingers moved slowly, ever lower, revealing the swell of one small breast above its tightly wrapped bonds.

Will's mouth watered; his teeth itched. He had to close his eyes so he could will his fangs back where they belonged. Even so, he cut his tongue, and the taste of his own blood filled his mouth. He thought he might pass out as every last drop seemed to race southward.

He breathed in, then out, then in again, and he could have sworn he caught the scent of—

Decay.

Will frowned. That wasn't right. He should be smelling roses.

He opened his eyes. Kate's gaze held his as she continued to open her doublet, and he forgot all about smelling anything.

Then he heard a shuffle to the rear. But they were alone. He had ordered everyone to stay gone until the time came for them to come back in.

Something had fallen; that was all. Fate would not be so cruel as to—

"Br," said a voice. "Br-br-brrrrrrrrr!!!"

Chapter Nineteen

"It seems she hangs upon the cheek of night
like a rich jewel in an Ethiope's ear."

—*Romeo and Juliet* (Act I, scene 5)

My eyes had been locked on Will's. When he'd closed his and breathed in and out several times, I'd been afraid he meant to deny me. And when he'd opened his eyes, his expression had at first been puzzled, his nose wrinkled like he'd smelled something foul.

My heart had taken a leap, as if I'd stepped off a cliff and paused high above my death; then it dropped when his face reflected the lust that must be all over my own.

He didn't care that my breasts were small and my skin was dun. In fact, he appeared to enjoy it.

Then I heard a scrape, saw movement in the shadows, opened my mouth to call out, *Who goes there?* but before I could utter a sound, another shot from the darkness.

"Br-br-brrrr!"

"Fate," Will muttered, "is a vicious, vicious bitch."

They came out of the gloom like an army. More than I could have handled alone. Praise God, Will was there.

He whirled, putting me behind him, but he had no weapon. I drew my sword, grabbed a handful of his doublet, and yanked him back. "Find a sword!" I shouted.

"I won't leave you."

"Now!" I swiped at the nearest zombie, which happened to be chanting "*Br-br-br!*" so loudly my mind fairly buzzed with it. The next instant he was ashes, and I could think again. "Go, Will. I can hold them off for a minute."

That he believed me and went caused a warm feeling to settle in my chest. He respected my ability, trusted me to do as I vowed despite my being a weak-willed woman. I wasn't used to that.

The zombies approached. They might possess gruel for brains, but they knew how to attack. I dispatched two that attempted to flank me.

Or perhaps their maker had merely instructed them what to do. I had no idea how zombies "worked"; I only knew that they did until I made them stop.

Footsteps from the rear caused me to duck, spin, swipe. I nearly skewered Will.

"Sorry!" I wasn't used to fighting with anyone but myself.

The zombies took advantage of my distraction and advanced. I managed to decapitate one that had made it onto the stage and shambled too near. Another stood just behind.

I would have dispatched him as well, except I slid in the ashes that had begun to coat the floor, and the zombie grabbed me, pinning my arms to my sides.

"Brrrr," he said, teeth snapping a mere inch from my nose.

"Kate!" Will shouted, worry coloring his voice.

I jerked my head back. "I'm all right."

I heard his step behind me, but he couldn't end the zombie without ending me. We were too close.

A woman couldn't be a hunter for very long and not find herself in difficult situations, so I did what I always did when trapped. I let my knees collapse; then I slithered from the zombie's grasp like a serpent.

Usually, I followed such a move with a kick that swept the fiend's feet out from under him, and when he landed next to me, I ended him.

Before I managed even the slightest movement, ashes rained down. I glanced up as Will's sword arced above my head. His gaze met mine.

"Thanks," I said, then bounded to my feet to greet the rest.

We fought back-to-back, me tending to the zombies at the front, Will tending to those that had wandered to the rear.

Their remains thickened the air and nearly covered the floor. Considering this was Will's first experience killing them, he did very well. In fact, he did so well I found it hard to believe he had not done it before.

He was amazingly quick and much, *much* stronger than he looked. One zombie was so tall I had to tilt my head to see his face, and he must have weighed nearly twenty-one stone since the floor creaked beneath his weight.

"Get off my stage!" Will shouted, and swung. The beast grabbed the sword and yanked.

I prepared to dive in and save Will Shakespeare's life. I needn't have worried. Will pulled his weapon free—I'm not sure how, considering the length and breadth and apparent strength of the tibonage—then hacked off the offending hand. The appendage dropped to the ground and began to crawl. Blood spurted everywhere.

"Off with the *head*," I muttered. I needn't have. Will dispatched the creature with a single backhanded blow while it was still trying to figure out where its hand had gone.

Both the zombie and the crawling disembodied piece of him burst into ashes.

The tibonage came at us for longer than I'd ever been come at before, but eventually there were none left to be killed. Will and I stood in the center of the very dirty stage and tried to catch our breath.

"Wh-wh-what," I managed, "was that?"

"Zombie attack," Will said, annoyingly unwinded.

I cast him an evil glare. "I know it was a zombie attack, but why?"

He frowned. "Why?"

"They're raised for a reason, Will. I doubt it was to kill us."

His frown deepened. "Yet they seemed so determined."

I lowered my gaze to the ashes swirling across the floor. "They did."

"We need to set things right before the others return," he said.

I glanced at him, surprised. I wanted to get to the bottom of the mystery; he didn't seem to care. But he was correct. We were as covered in zombie ash as the stage. If we planned to avoid questions we could not answer, we must get rid of the evidence. Time enough to solve the mystery later.

"I'll take care of this." Will waved at the mess that eddied all around us. "Use the tiring room to wash."

"I can—" I began.

"Go!" he ordered.

Something in his face made me comply.

The Rose felt deserted, though if there was a zombie hiding behind a bit of scenery, would I discover that before the fiend leaped out and tried to eat me? Doubtful.

But I'd never known zombies to have the *br—* to hide. They came at you. It was what they did.

So I went to the tiring room without bothering to search the wings, however, I kept my sword in my hand and my gaze sharp on the shadows.

Within that space, I found clear, cool water and cloths. As I took off my doublet, zombie ash sprinkled down. My hair was full of it, my face, no doubt, a mask of grime.

I wet a square of material and swiped it over my cheeks and neck. "Ah," I murmured. "Heavenly." I was not only grimy but sweaty. Not attractive in the least.

The thought caused a sound of impatience to erupt from my lips, followed by a chastisement that might have come from Nounou herself. "What care you if you are pretty in this moment? You are a chasseur. Better to be filthy with the remains of the evil ones than the most beautiful dead woman in London."

I continued to wipe the cool, damp cloth over my filthy skin. Having been in the process of removing my doublet when the attack came, I now had ashes everywhere. At least I would not need to lie to Nurse as to why my bathwater had turned black when all I'd done was sleep. More and more I wondered why I hadn't locked her up years ago.

I wandered to Will's desk and discovered page upon page covered with scrawls. I picked one up and read: "In the old age black was not counted fair, or if it were, it bore not beauty's name."

Lifting my hand, I let my fingers trail through my black tresses as I continued to read. "Therefore my mistress' eyes are raven black, her eyes so suited, and they mourners seem at such who, not born fair, no beauty lack, sland'ring creation with a false esteem."

I set the paper on the desk and touched the lids of my raven black eyes.

"Yet so they mourn, becoming of their woe"—I spun about. Will stood in the doorway—"that every tongue says beauty should look so."

If I'd had any doubt the sonnet was about me, that doubt died with the expression on his face.

"When did you write that?" I managed.

"The instant I first saw you."

I smiled. "Liar."

He lifted one shoulder, and ashes cascaded to the ground. "Near enough. From the moment I met you, sweet Kate, there weren't enough hours in the day to write down all the words tumbling through my head."

"By what I've heard, words tumble into your head much more regularly than they tumble into any other playwright's in England. They say you could not have written alone all that you have written."

"They say many things." He inched ever closer. "Pray do not believe them."

Will's gaze wandered lower and flared hot. I suddenly realized I stood before him in nothing but my breeches and the bindings over my breasts. I reached for the dirty doublet, and Will lifted a hand to stay me.

"Wait." He licked his lips, pressed them together, lifted his eyes. "Please. Just another moment, I hear—"

I tensed, thinking more zombies on their way, until he whispered, "The sonnet. Shhh."

Though he continued to stare at my breasts, such that they were, his eyes went unfocused, and I wondered if he saw them, or me, at all.

He began to speak, words of such beauty my eyes stung with unshed tears. No one had ever seen me the way that Will Shakespeare did, and I knew in that instant that no one ever would.

Chapter Twenty

"I bear a charmed life."
—*Macbeth* (Act V, scene 8)

The words, they poured into Will's head, so many he thought he might burst.

He could not take his gaze from Kate, the shade of her skin dark against the stark white of the bonds across her breasts. He wanted to tear those bonds loose with his fangs, then lick the flesh beneath like dessert.

His teeth itched abominably, and he tightened his lips, then focused on the poetry in his mind. "My mistress' eyes are nothing like the sun," he muttered. "Red her lips. No. Too common." He focused on Kate's sweet, full mouth. "Coral. Yes. Coral is far more red than her lips' red."

Those lips curved, and he wanted to take them with his own, to bite them just a little until the blood that pulsed beneath the surface made them redder still. She would taste of grapes ripening beneath the sun and lust the shade of flames.

Her breathing quickened along with his own, causing the slope of her breasts to rise and fall, an enticement even to one less weak than he.

"If snow be white, why then her breasts are dun. If hairs be wires, black wires grow on her head."

Those coral lips turned down, and her breath caught.

"No," he said, and waved the words away before she could protest. What woman would like her hair described as wire? He needed something prettier, but for now it would do. Time to rewrite in the dark of the night as the world all around him slept.

"Roses," he blurted, and she tilted her head. "I have seen roses damasked, red and white, but no such roses see I in her cheeks."

Will moved closer, drawn by the earthy scent of her. He stood a hairsbreadth away, and she tilted her exquisite face to his. When her breath wafted over him, he fair got a headache with the flash of the words through his brain.

"And in some perfumes is there more delight than in the breath that from my mistress reeks."

She blinked. Maybe not *reeks*. Something else. But that for later.

Her eyes were black, and right now one was blacker still. He had not gotten to the bottom of that yet, but he would. 'Twould be for later as well.

"Will," she whispered. "I—"

He reached for his quill, scrabbled for an empty piece of paper. "Hold," he ordered. "But soft—" He lifted his finger and quickly wrote all he could recall of the sonnet to his Dark Lady.

When he was done, he paused. "I must speak of your voice, which haunts me in my dreams. The way you walk. The rarity of my love."

"Your love *'tis* rare," she muttered. "'Tis ridiculous to say you love me."

He blinked, and the lingering words disappeared. "I do."

"Will," she began again.

"Kate," he interrupted. "You have given me back my voice. For that alone I would love you into eternity."

And for him eternity was very, very real.

"You're a fool," she said.

"I have been called worse."

Her dark, slim, arched brows lifted. "Who dares?"

Will laughed. "Would you fight them for me, sweet Kate?"

"Unto the end of my days."

His heart stuttered. For an instant he thought it might beat. God's blood, he actually *did* love her.

Bloody hell! He knew better. Humans died. Dying was what they did best.

The idea of Kate—pale and still—gone, nearly sent him to his knees. He had to turn away so she did not see the horror in his eyes and the agony upon his face. She wouldn't understand.

He didn't.

Men like him bandied the word *love* about all the time. He went from woman to woman, scribbling what he felt, what he saw, what he tasted.

He was a writer. He could not help himself.

But Kate . . . Kate was different.

She would be the death of him—if not literally, then figuratively when his soul flew along with her to the grave.

"Lovely," he murmured. "I should write that down."

"Will!" Kate had her hands on her hips and fury in her eyes. She was so beautiful.

"I just told you I would protect you to the end of my days, and off you go into your head."

"I do that."

"I noticed." Her lips curved. "It is what makes you you. I understand."

He thought that she just might, and that thought only made him adore her all the more.

His gaze was drawn again to her breasts. She stood in front of him as if she were fully clothed instead of nigh onto naked. Her lack of embarrassment only inflamed him further. He could fair taste that skin, the shade of the earth framing bonds as white as the caps upon the sea. She would taste of salt like that sea, and her blood—

Will brought himself up short. He could not taste her blood. For if he did, he would never be able to stop.

"I am not your mistress," she said.

His eyes lifted to hers. He could not fathom the expression he saw there. "The words," he said. "They come, and I cannot change them. Until later. Rewrites." He shrugged. "A writer's privilege."

"I just hate to—" She paused.

Will waited for her to say that she would not see her name slandered in print, that a baseborn playwright was not fit to use her likeness so callously.

If she asked him not to publish the sonnet, would he acquiesce? Already he knew it was some of the best work he'd ever done.

"Lie," she said.

"What?" Had he lied? Of course. But which lie was she talking about?

"I hate to lie," she repeated slowly, as if talking to an imbecile.

Understanding dawned, and Will could barely breathe. Lucky he did not need to.

She stepped closer. "Make your lie the truth, Will." She lifted her coral lips to his. "Give me my sin again."

He kicked shut the door, then he did.

Chapter Twenty-one

"For ever and a day."

—*As You Like It* (Act IV, scene I)

How could I resist a man who spoke words of saintly beauty through lips that tasted of sin? Or the way he looked at me, the way he touched me, the way he kissed me—

Ah, his kisses. They were like brandy-wine—sweet and strong. Intoxicating. Addicting. I'd known from the very first that I would never be able to get enough.

His mouth was soft, the kiss quite hard, his hands at my waist so cool. His palms supple, but his fingertips scraped. I shivered at the contrast of sensations.

He lifted his head. "Cold?"

I shook mine, lips reaching for his. But his gaze was caught on something much lower than my face. I followed it.

My breasts? He seemed inordinately fascinated with them. Which only endeared him to me more.

Slowly he raised his hand, ran a rough fingertip across the virgin swell. I gasped as that one slight touch shot through me like a cannon through a precious spring morn.

"Does this hurt?" He lowered his head and licked the red mark left by the too-tight bonds.

Hurt? I sighed, the sound pure arousal. *Yes. And then again no.*

When his tongue dipped in the valley, I shuddered and arched and begged without words for more.

"It is a sin to taint such beauty with a torturous twist." His breath cascaded over the damp trail left by his mouth. My body clenched, my entire being waiting, wanting, willing.

He tugged on the bindings, but I'd sweated them through, then gotten them dirty and wet again with the water from his basin. No wonder they'd marked me. The linen had fair shrunk to a size fit for a child.

Disappointment flourished. I wanted him to touch me, everywhere. But I'd have to cut the bindings away. They would not unravel without aid. And I didn't want to leave his embrace, not even for the few moments it would take to release myself.

Suddenly, Will cursed and bent at the waist. Both the words and the movement were so violent I stepped back— just in time to watch him remove a dagger from his boot with a quick, practiced flick. As he straightened, he flipped the weapon end over end, catching it adroitly and bringing the tip down upon the northernmost edge of the cloth.

His gaze met mine; my breathing quickened as my body melted on a sudden wave of heat. One instant he was a dreamy-eyed writer spouting poetry to my dun-shaded breasts, and the next he was a warrior, drawing a concealed weapon to release those breasts from captivity. What other secrets did this man have, and would I live long enough to discover them?

He lifted one brow, and his fine lips quirked, a question for which there was only one answer.

"Please," I whispered, and he cut the bindings from my skin.

They'd drawn in so tightly, my breasts fair bounced free, quite the feat considering. A tiny sharp pain speared, nothing compared to the sensation of cool, whirling air upon them.

The clatter of the dagger; Will's gasp made my gaze flick to his. He stared at my chest, expression full of horror, and my face heated.

I'd been told I was ugly. Too dark, too thin, too *me* for any man to adore. I'd believed Reginald when he'd spoken his loving lies only to have my heart crushed by the truth.

But apparently not crushed enough, as I'd gone and trusted Will too. I'd believed him when he said I was beautiful. The expression on his face told me differently.

I covered myself with my arms, began to turn away, eyes searching for something, anything to throw over my nakedness as I ran for home.

"No," he said, his voice choked. "I'm sorry. I didn't mean—"

"You can't help how you feel. I know I'm not the fashion."

"What?"

I sensed him glance at me. "Oh, God, Kate, no. You are the loveliest creature I've ever seen. Do not cover yourself like that." His rough-soft hand brushed my shoulder. "Do not *ever* cover yourself with me."

"I cannot—"

"I cut you!" His voice was agonized. "There's—" He swallowed thickly as if he might be sick. "Blood."

A thin trickle of red ran across the hills and valleys of my ribs. Nothing to be so alarmed about. I bled worse than that of a month.

So sensitive. Poor man. I supposed he felt more deeply than most. He would have to in order to write the way he did. Most likely he'd experienced the sharp slice of the dagger like a cut to his own heart while I'd barely noticed.

"I'm all right, Will. 'Tis nothing." I snatched a clean cloth and wiped the blood away. After a few pats, the bleeding stopped.

He'd turned his face to the door, his shoulders tense, hands clenched. I touched his shoulder again, and he flinched. "Do not look at me."

"Why?"

He breathed in and out, short and quick, as if he'd run a long, long way. He said nothing for so long, I did not think he would answer, then, voice hoarse, he spoke. "C-close your eyes, sweet Kate. Let me kiss you as if we lived in the dark."

"I do not understand."

"I cannot—" he muttered. "I must—"

"I'm all *right,* Will."

"Please, Kate, do as I ask, or I must go."

"You will *not* leave me so unsatisfied," I snapped.

His breath came, both hard and shaky. "Oh blessed, blessed night! I am—" He paused, his hands clenching again as if he were fighting something no one else could see. "Afraid," he blurted, the word sounding as if it were pulled from him in pain and blood. "I am afraid that by being in night, all this is but a dream. Too flattering-sweet to be substantial. If I stare in your eyes, and I see it isn't real—"

"Hush," I said, and touched him again. This time he did not flinch but rather stilled. "Whatever you wish, you have only to ask. Be not afraid. This is real, Will, and I am here."

I closed my eyes and let him kiss me as if it were the darkest of night and we the only beings in this world.

His lips so cool on my feverish mouth, I drank him in like a chill autumn mist, pressed into him as if I might crawl within and pull him around me like a warmed blanket in the midst of a winter storm.

I must have pressed too hard, for I could have sworn his teeth scraped my lips as sharply as the dagger he'd dropped on the floor.

My eyes opened. His stared into mine; I could not read his expression. When I licked my lip to see if it bled, his gaze lowered and locked on my tongue.

Then he was kissing me, touching me, pulling the rest of my clothes from my body as he backed me toward the long bench in the corner of the room.

Only now that we needed one did I see there was no bed. How strange. Although this wasn't a home, no matter that Will seemed to live here.

The back of my legs struck the bench, and I sat down hard, my lips coming unstuck from Will's with a loud *smack*. His mouth appeared ravaged. Had I done that? The sight enflamed me, and I reached for him, palming his fullness, then running a fingertip along his length.

He drew in a sharp breath and grasped my wrist. I lifted my eyes. "Did I hurt you?"

His mouth quirked. "Hurt me again, Dark Lady." I tugged on my arm, but he tightened his hold. "Later. Right now, if you continue in that vein, you will unman me."

That I could have such an effect with a simple touch made

my blood first flow fast with heat, then thud slowly down low.

His eyes flared as if he sensed my reaction. How could that be? Then my gaze fell on his hand, where his fingertips lay against the pulse at my wrist.

He lifted my arm, pressed his lips to that wrist. His tongue flicked out, laved the beating vein; his teeth grazed it, and for just an instant I had a flash of what it would feel like if he bit me, if he drank from me.

Oddly, I wanted him to.

I shook my head hard, and that longing went away.

"Kate?" Will murmured. "Is something amiss?"

Was it? No. Merely the mind of a hunter haunted by the monster she must hunt. It happened, though never before in this situation. Perhaps because I'd never been in this situation—my body so aroused, my mind so tightly wound I thought I might burst if he kissed me again.

"Kate?" Will dropped my arm, stepped back.

"No!" I reached for him, drew him down upon me. "Nothing is amiss; nothing will be amiss unless you leave me now."

Desperate, a bit frightened—and the last almost brought laughter—frightened that he might not touch me, might not take me, I who faced the tibonage and my own death nearly every night. I would think myself a fool if not for the very real tremble in my hands.

His clothes melted away; his skin slid along mine. How could he be so cool? Mayhap because he had done this a thousand times before.

Fury made me flush, but I forced it away. What went before mattered not. I of all people should know that.

And I liked his cool skin, his smooth back, his taut . . . places. Those contrasts, soft and hard, smooth and rough, hill and valley, intrigued me. I wound my ankle around his like the sinuous tail of a cat, the movement causing his body to rest exactly where it belonged.

"Mmm," I murmured, and arched like that cat.

He was all long legs and slim hips. Muscles rippled beneath my hands, and I followed their trail with my fingertips. Those muscles were as long and lean as the rest of him. He was so much stronger than he looked, than he felt. Another intriguing mystery to add to the man. But that was for later.

He lifted those slim hips and slipped within.

Much later.

As if all holds upon him had broken, he surged and retreated like the waves of the ocean in the heat of a summer storm. Cold upon hot, wet and wetter still, hard into soft, again and again and again.

His mouth at my breast so cool, the pull on my nipple so sharp I cried out, and he laved the tender hurt, suckling like a babe. Somewhere in the distant night a cry, my own voice perhaps, yet I was so beside myself, so wound up in him, I couldn't be sure.

He pulled me tighter against him, plunged deeper within. Needing to hold on, I wrapped my legs, my arms about him.

"Kiss me, Kate," he murmured into my neck, and when I did, he pulsed, hot and cold, dark and light, night and day, man and woman, the way it should be.

His seed so hot it felt like ice, the pleasure so deep it seemed like pain. I gasped and grasped, held on, never wanting this to end, but one shift of my body was all it took for me to pulse as well.

I'd never pulsed before. I quite enjoyed it.

When both our ardor and our bodies had cooled, Will brushed my tangled hair from my damp face. "I will leave you never, sweet Kate." He lowered his head until his lips hovered a mere breath from mine. "Never," he said again, then, "forever."

Those words became a pledge more binding than any vow I'd ever known.

Chapter Twenty-two

"Love sought is good, but giv'n unsought is better."
—*Twelfth Night* (Act III, scene 1)

What had he done?

Touched her. Kissed her. Loved her.

Made love to her. His Kate. Who was not truly his at all.

Will pulled her to his side, stilled as her breath wafted across his chest. If this was the one time, the only time that they had, he would keep her in his arms for as long as he could.

"Ah, Will," she sighed. "That was . . ."

He waited; she did not finish. "Was . . . ?" he prompted.

"I did not know. I never could have imagined how it would be. How *we* could be. Together." She laid her hand on his hip, ran her thumb along the bone that lay beneath. "I enjoyed lying."

"Lying?" he repeated, and his voice shook like a child's.

She cuddled closer. "By your side."

Word play. Usually he was better at it than most, but right now—

Will's teeth ground together. "Speak plainly, Kate, afore I lose my mind."

She peered into his face, recognized his concern, and smiled. "Will, I understand now what all those sonnets are about."

He let out the breath he'd held, forced his jaw to release its grip upon his teeth. He'd been told he was an amazing lover—he ought to be, he'd practiced for centuries—but Kate was different.

Kate he loved.

Therefore, the loving should be different, and it had been. For him. He'd wanted it badly to be different for her. From her gasps and sighs, he'd believed it so. Then again, she was nearly as good a performer as he.

Kate came up on her elbow, staring into his eyes as her hair cascaded across his chest. He wanted her again, but he dared not say. A *man* could not manage so soon. Not that she would know . . .

"I'm thirsty," she whispered, and kissed him, drinking from his lips as if they were the only water left upon a dying and parched earth.

Her taste, her touch, they made him feel and think and need. He found the words again, and when she lifted her head, they poured free. "Till, breathless, he disjoin'd, and backward drew. The heavenly moisture, that sweet coral mouth"—he traced it with his fingernail, scraping just enough to make her moan—"whose precious taste her thirsty lips well knew."

"Her lips are conquerors," she whispered, "his lips obey."

"Beautiful," Will breathed. He must use it. "Now quick desire hath caught the yielding prey, and glutton-like she feeds, yet never filleth."

"Are you calling me a glutton?" she asked, but her voice, her face, was full of laughter. She didn't wait for him to answer. "You'd be right. I doubt I'll ever get enough of the taste of your skin, Will Shakespeare."

And with that she began to kiss his chest, lick his neck, test her teeth upon his—

Zounds! Where had she learned that?

She gave him his sin again, and it was good. Better than good. He never wanted to leave this bench, this room, this woman.

But he must.

"They'll return soon," he murmured.

"Mmm," she said.

"If they find us here—"

"They will murder us," she muttered, half-asleep.

She remembered the words they'd said to each other that first night. Words he'd already set down on paper as one scene in a future play. Warring families. Venice. No! Verona. Love and hate, life and death.

The usual.

On one side her sooty lashes lay stark against the lighter shade of her face. Beneath the other those dark lashes disappeared when set against the plum-colored skin of the bruise.

Gently, he slid his finger across it, and she hissed, her eyes snapping open. "Who did this to you?" he asked.

"I told you. 'Twas an accident."

"Your nurse kicked you."

"Yes."

"You are certain your—" He paused, not wanting to say the word, to bring the man between them, but he had to. "Husband," he blurted. "He has not returned?"

She laughed. "He would not dare to touch me thus. He has seen me with a rapier."

Will's lip quirked. What a woman she was! Everything about her intrigued him.

"If he discovers you gone, that you have been here, with me—"

A shadow flitted through her eyes, and Will's amusement fled. If the man ever put a mark on her, he would meet with a very bloody accident.

"I do not know what he will do. But I could no more remain safe inside with the tibonage free to roam than I could—" She hesitated.

"Than you could what?" he murmured.

She didn't speak for several seconds, and when she did he had the impression she had meant to say something else. "Than I could endure Nurse's hovering one day longer."

"So you confined her."

"If I had not, I wouldn't be here now."

Will thought about that. "Fine." He gave a sharp nod. "Confine her."

"You do not want to know why?"

"No. As long as you are here, and you come back, I do not care what you do." To her nurse or anyone else.

"I can't be with you forever, Will." She took his hand. "This *isn't* forever."

He stared into her endless eyes. "You have no idea what forever means."

She dropped his hand, stood, and began to pin her hair beneath her cap. Damnation, he was a fool!

"I think I do," she said tightly. "I am pledged forever to a man I loathe while the man I—" Her voice broke. She bent over and snatched her doublet from the floor. Ashes flew when she shook it furiously.

Will got up and crossed the short distance between them. He did not touch her. He could not. "The man you what, Kate?"

Her eyes said it all. She loved him; he knew it. She opened her mouth to speak, to tell him the only words he'd never heard in all of his long, lonely lives.

And there was a knock on his door.

Chapter Twenty-three

"There is nothing either good or
bad, but thinking makes it so."

—*Hamlet* (Act II, scene 2)

Thank the Lord for Edmond. He kept me from foolishly
telling Will that I loved him. Certainly he'd said the same to
me, but I didn't believe him. He was a poet; he spouted love
like he spouted . . . well, poetry.

"Master Shakespeare?" Edmond knocked again. "Sir? It is
time for rehearsal. Be ye there?"

"Yes, Edmond, I– "

Edmond walked in.

I was in the process of putting on my doublet and yanked
it over my nakedness so quickly I laid a long scratch across
my belly and cursed. The words drew Edmond's attention
directly to me.

His widened, and his cheeks reddened. His gaze went to
the floor and stayed there as he backed out of the room, then
shut the door behind him.

I peered into the mirror that hung upon the wall. My hair

was up; my cap was on; I could pass for a boy. I stepped back, and my eyes lowered to my doublet.

Except for my breasts.

I cursed some more. I didn't have much, but I had enough that I would not be taken for a boy if anyone were inclined to look.

"He knows," I said.

"That we are lovers?" Will rubbed his forehead. "I believe everyone knows. Or will soon enough."

"He knows I'm a woman."

Will dropped his hand, frowned. "How so?"

I waved vaguely at my breasts, and Will laughed. "No, sweet Kate, I do not think Edmond saw you long enough to notice." His laughter died. "Which is lucky for him."

For an instant, the expression on Will's face scared me. He appeared fierce, primal, an animal protecting his mate. Then the expression was gone, and he was just Will again. Handsome, dashing, brilliant Will.

"Edmond thinks us *male* lovers?" I asked.

"Yes." Will glanced at the closed door.

"Is that a problem?"

"It isn't anything Edmond hasn't seen before."

"With you?"

"No!" I jumped at his ferocity, and he took a deep breath, relaxing as he released it. "Not that there's anything wrong with it. Men just aren't something I've ever been interested in . . . in that way." His gaze upon me softened. "So innocent, my sweet Kate."

I lifted my chin. "Not as innocent as you think."

"No." He glanced at my mouth, and his eyes darkened. I

knew he was remembering where so recently that mouth had been. "Not so innocent," he agreed.

The way he looked at me made me want him again. It was as if he'd cast a spell. How could I feel so much so quickly? Merely because of how his hands caressed my skin and his lips caressed my body?

Perhaps. I smiled to myself, caught a glimpse of the expression in the mirror, and smiled even more. I'd seen that expression on many a woman's face and always wondered what it meant. Now I knew. I knew so many things now that I'd never imagined before.

"I will need help," I said.

Will, in the midst of dressing himself, paused. "Help?" he repeated.

"To bind my breasts. You destroyed the wrappings." The memory made my breath come faster, my breasts rise and fall so quickly they drew Will's attention like a solitary ship bobbing on a clear blue sea.

"Yes," he agreed, gaze stuck to my chest. "I will have to help.

"Do you have something we could use for a binding?"

"Binding," he repeated, then shook his head hard. "Yes. One moment."

He began to root through a pile of clothing in the corner, which gave me time to enjoy the warm, womanly glow in my belly. To make a man so crazy with love just by the sight of you . . . it meant something. I wasn't exactly sure what, but I liked it.

"Here!" Will yanked out a long piece of red cloth. "We were going to use this for a flag in one of the history plays but—" Will frowned. "We didn't. I can't recall why."

He was so adorably forgetful. I loved it when his eyes glossed over, and his face went a little slack as he listened to the genius in his head and not to me. Perhaps some women would be angry, annoyed, even jealous, but as had been previously established, I was not "some women." I wasn't even "most women."

Will was who he was, and I—

Didn't want to think about that. If I admitted even to myself what I felt, I'd only get my heart broken when this ended.

And it had to end. Eventually.

"'Tis fine," I blurted. "Good. We'd better get to rehearsal before someone else comes knocking."

Will glanced up from the red cloth and gave one short, sharp burst of laughter. "I doubt anyone else will come knocking."

My face flamed. They wouldn't come knocking because they'd think we were—

"Take that off," Will ordered.

I blinked. Was he thinking the same thing? Did we have time?

However, when I peered into his face, he was intent on the red cloth, measuring the length, the width with his hands. I became breathless just watching him pet the cloth as he'd so recently petted me.

"Stop," I muttered, and yanked off the doublet.

"Hmm?" Will said.

I didn't answer; he wasn't paying attention anyway.

Instead, I lifted my arms above my head, and he leaned in, wrapping the fabric round and round. His fingertips brushed the swell; his knuckles grazed my nipples as his breath tickled my collarbone.

"Tighter," I said, and something in my voice must have called him back from wherever it was that he'd gone.

Will's gaze lifted slowly, traveling from my scarlet-bound breasts, past the quivering flesh of my shoulders and neck, to my face. Then he was kissing me, desperately, thoroughly, even as the bindings fell to the floor.

I guess we had time. No one came knocking.

A short while later, Will pulled the cloth so tight that all I could think of was finishing rehearsal and getting home so I could take it off.

"I have to write a new play for us to rehearse," Will muttered. "We have done *Henry VI* to death."

A snort of laughter escaped me, and Will glanced up. "Henry VI *was* done to death. By Richard."

"Very good." Will enjoyed clever word twists almost as much as he enjoyed me. "Think you what I've been hearing in my head might be the beginnings of a new play?"

I fastened my doublet over the red fabric and thought back to what he'd shared. "Touch but my lips with those fair lips of thine?" I asked.

"Look in mine eye balls," he replied, "there thy beauty lies; then why not lips on lips since eyes on eyes?"

"Beautiful, Will." I took his hand. "Really. But—"

He stiffened and withdrew his hand. "But?"

I must tread softly here and not stomp upon his artist's soul. But he had asked, so I answered.

"There is no story. Nothing to hold a play together. I hear a poem."

His face became thoughtful. "A sonnet?"

"Perhaps. Although I would not want the work to end so soon."

Will turned away, fastening his own doublet. "An epic, methinks. I've always wanted to write one."

He wandered out the door ahead of me, already lost in his new idea.

Chapter Twenty-four

"I am a man more sinned against than sinning."
—*King Lear* (Act III, scene 2)

Edward Alleyn was unamused to discover that Will did not have a new play in hand. Will attempted to placate him by reciting the best lines from his poem, but Ned was in no mood to hear.

"William, I do not care about a sonnet!"

"Epic," Will muttered, only to earn a glare from the man, and a glare from Edward Alleyn was quite intimidating. If Will hadn't been a secret, immortal vampire, he might have been scared.

Alleyn was one of the greatest actors of their time, and while Will often felt the man was an overblown braggart, his opinion was not shared by the masses. Taller than most, with a long, bearded face that could by turns reflect extreme joy and everlasting sorrow, Ned's deep, commanding voice would reach to every corner of the Rose with little effort on his part.

"Something shall come to me," Will said. "It always does."

"*How* does it come to you?" Ned asked.

"If I knew that, it would no longer come."

His words earned him another scowl. "Can you make it come faster? I'll pay you more."

"It does not work that way. But I'll think of something soon."

"See that you do, or I can have Kit Marlowe do so in a trice."

Will turned away so Ned would not see his smile. Alleyn used that threat often. Ned's father-in-law, Philip Henslowe, with whom Ned owned many business ventures, and Kit Marlowe were close. Many of Marlowe's plays had been first performed on this stage. What they didn't know was that Will had written those too.

Not that Kit couldn't write. He could, and well. He just lost interest after a few scenes, went out, got drunk, found a young man, and disappeared for days, sometimes weeks. By then Kit's passion for the story was gone.

The collaboration had begun one night when Will had dragged Kit home and poured him into his bed following a long eve of drunken debauchery. Will had discovered a half-finished play on the floor, and when Kit woke up the next day, Will had finished it. They agreed to keep that information just between them.

So now whenever Kit needed money but couldn't finish his work, Will did. Will didn't mind letting Marlowe take the credit as long as Will got paid. Living forever was expensive!

If people found out how many plays Will had actually written over the years, no one would believe they were all his. Best to let someone he liked and admired claim a few.

Kate waited in the wings. They'd rehearsed *Henry VI*

again. The only one who might have needed practice was Kate—the rest of them had performed the play more times than any of them cared to count—but she'd been perfect, as if she too had performed the play until it nauseated her.

Ned was right. The time for a new act was now.

Will had asked Kate to wait for him. He would walk her home. Certainly she was a chasseur, but with the number of zombies wandering the London streets, Will did not want her fighting them alone. She'd asked for his help, and he would give it to her.

"Your boy awaits you," Ned murmured.

Though Will did not like the way Ned said "your boy," he merely nodded and continued on.

"You'd best hope your wife does not find out."

Will stopped and turned. "And how would that happen, Ned? My wife lives in Stratford."

"Convenient."

"Very." Especially since she wasn't really his wife.

"You don't have the time to spare for a new lover right now. You have a play to write."

"And write it I will. Have no fear."

Will strode away fuming. Who he spent time with was no one's business. Certainly not Ned's.

However, he didn't want Anne to find out. He would not have her hurt. Will had vowed to protect and care for her, and he would. For all the rest of her days.

He could barely remember what his name had been when he'd been born, but it hadn't been William Shakespeare. He'd taken that name not five years past from a poor, sorry chap who'd died in his arms, the victim of a robbery gone bad.

The night had been foggy, as London nights often were, and Will had been wandering the streets when suddenly—

"'Tis all that I have. If I give it to you, my children will starve."

"Better yours than mine. Give over."

"No."

The word had been stated with utter conviction, and Will had hurried forward, intent not only on giving aid but also on seeing the man who'd spoken it. But he was too late.

A cry, the dull thud of a body hitting the street, and the sweet, fresh scent of blood.

He lay in a spreading red puddle, a deep knife wound to his belly. Will considered giving chase, but what good would it do? Apprehending the thief would not save this man. Only he could.

"Friend, I can give you eternal life."

"Eternal?" the true Shakespeare murmured, then coughed, blood bubbling upon his lips. "I doubt that."

"As long as you take care to avoid sharp objects slicing through your neck. And bright sunlight."

"I could not live without the sun," the fellow whispered.

Will forced his fangs back where they belonged.

He sat with the chap as his life ebbed away, and he noticed that they resembled each other greatly. The first Will begged the second to look after his wife and three small children. And that was when the vampire had an idea . . .

He'd wandered the world without a home or a family. He wanted a name. A life. A past. He could have one. All he need do was make, and keep, a promise to a dying man.

So he did.

As Will drew nearer to Kate, he searched her face, wondering if she'd heard the conversation with Ned. He didn't want to lie to her any more than he already had, and he wouldn't. If she asked about Anne, he'd tell her. About the children too. He just hoped that she wouldn't ask.

Her expression was welcoming, no annoyance, not a hint of curiosity. "You do not have to walk me home, Will," she said lowly. "I've been out alone in the night for years."

"You do not have to be alone any longer," he said, and took her hand. A glance over his shoulder revealed Ned still watching them. Will lifted a brow, and at last Alleyn turned away.

"Why is Mr. Alleyn angry?" she asked. "Because of us?"

"No." That wasn't a lie. Exactly. "He wants a new play, and he wants it now."

They stepped into the cool, damp air of a London autumn eve. The stars fair twinkled, and the moon was full. In that light, Kate's skin glowed like candle flame upon the water, and Will could no longer see the bruise beneath her eye. Words spun wickedly through his head, making him dizzy.

So oft have I invoked thee for my Muse, and found such fair assistance in my verse, as every—

Kate laughed, and any other words there might have been flew away on the music of her mirth. "Edward Alleyn of all people should understand how creativity works."

"How does it work?" Will asked.

"I—" She paused. "Have no idea. Do you?"

"No. For weeks I couldn't write a word. Then you come into my life, and I cannot seem to stop."

"I bet you say that to all the boys," Kate murmured.

———

They reached the manor house without incident. Had they dispatched all the zombies in London?

Even if they had, there would be more. Unless the fiends had somehow accomplished their nefarious purpose. Whatever it was.

Somehow Will doubted that. He hadn't heard of any large fight, a mass murder, an assassination. For there to be so many zombies gamboling about, something big was about to happen.

Big and bad.

Enchanted by the scent of Kate, the sight of her, the feel of her next to, and beneath, him, Will had been lax in his duties. He should have followed one of the fiends back to his maker and discovered who it was and what the necro-vampire was after. Then Will could dispatch him.

Without a maker to give orders, the zombies would be lost. Easy prey for two such as Will and Kate. Not that they weren't already.

Will expected to climb the trellis onto Kate's balcony as he had the last time he'd been here. Instead, she shocked him by walking in the front door. A moment later her head popped out. "Will you come in?"

He stared at the great house, half-expecting a footman or a butler to shoo him away. "I'd best not," he said.

"I need to ask you something." She went in. A moment later, she came out again. "Will!"

"But . . . the servants."

"Have all run off. They believe my nurse has the plague."

The manor was well furnished, well lit. Clean. Will had been in such houses but only as the entertainment. Which wasn't much different from his position right now.

Will wasn't a fool. This was England. Old King Hal might divorce whomever he pleased, but that didn't mean anyone else could do it. Certainly not a wealthy merchant's daughter.

Will put those thoughts from his mind. What good did they do? Did he plan to leave her? Never to see her again? No. He'd rather step into the bright light of the morning sun than live without his sweet Kate and the words she had brought back into his life.

Chapter Twenty-five

"Look like the innocent flower,
but be the serpent under 't."

—*Macbeth* (Act I, scene 5)

Will stared at the wallpaper, the rugs, the furniture as if he'd never seen the like before. Maybe he hadn't.

For an instant, I felt embarrassed by my wealth, uneasy about the difference in our stations. But not because he had nothing, and I had everything. In my opinion, our situations were just the opposite.

"Your room?" Will asked.

"My room?" I frowned. "She isn't there."

Will had already set one foot on the steps that led to the living quarters. "She?"

"My nurse."

"You brought me here to—" He paused. "I thought—"

He glanced upward again. He'd thought I had brought him here to— My own gaze rested momentarily on the door to my suite.

I took his hand. "Maybe later," I said. Then I tugged him through the house and toward the stables.

"What can *I* do for your nurse, Kate?"

"She isn't really sick," I said.

"I gathered that, as you don't seem overly concerned about tending her. Once again, what can I do?"

"Tell her she's ill, that she must remain abed. Until you allow otherwise."

"Me, but I'm just a lowly—" He paused, and understanding dawned. "Actor," he finished.

Will Shakespeare was nothing if not quick.

His head tilted, and for an instant I thought he'd heard Nurse banging on the walls of her prison. Except she wasn't.

Jamie appeared. The smile that had spread across his face when he saw me turned to a scowl when he saw Will. "Who're you?" he demanded.

I opened my mouth, but Will spoke first. With a French accent. And a very bad one at that.

"*Oui,* I am Dr. Caius. And who might you be, *jeune homme?*"

Jamie looked at me. "What the heck kind of doctor is he? Cain't understand half of what he's sayin'."

I gave Will a narrow glare. "This is Jamie, Doctor. He's my stable hand. Jamie, how is our good nurse today?"

"Loud," Jamie muttered. "Till about an hour past. Then she shut up right quick." His face brightened beneath the shaggy mop of his yellow-white hair. "Ye think she died?"

"Ach," Will said. "Dis is vy I have come. To make sure de lady does not leave dis vorld too soon."

He sounded like a German attempting to murder the French language. I had no idea what he was up to, but I also had no choice but to move forward with our ruse.

"Could you run and have Cook pour some wine, Jamie?"

"Wine?" Will spat on the ground. "English wine is swill."

Jamie's hands curled into fists. I didn't blame the lad. Will was asking for a good thrashing.

"English wine is all we've got, *Doctor.*" Jamie gave the last word a snooty little twist, mocking the man. Will's eyebrows lifted, and his lips twitched.

"Perhaps some bread and honey as well." I set my hands on Jamie's shoulders, then turned the boy toward the house and gave him a little shove. "Go."

I waited until he'd disappeared inside before drawing Will within.

"He has a fine ear for mimicry," Will said in the voice I knew so well. How could he switch back and forth without a thought? "I could use him at the Rose."

"Oh, no. He's the only stable hand I have, Will Shakespeare. You leave him be."

I felt protective of Jamie. The boy had stayed when everyone else had left, and for that he would be rewarded. But not with a lifetime in the theater. Such a life was for those who lived and breathed nothing else. From what I'd observed, Jamie lived and breathed horse.

Will continued to stare at the door through which Jamie would reappear although he didn't seem to see it. He'd gone off into his own world again, and, really, we just didn't have the time.

"Will!"

"Hmm?" His attention shifted to my face, and for an instant I could have sworn he did not recognize me. I very nearly asked what he'd seen, what he'd heard; then his gaze cleared, and he was back with me, warmth flooding his ebony eyes. "Show me de vay, *chérie.*"

"Must you speak with that atrocious accent?"

"You do not like it?"

"It grates upon the ear."

"Good." He grinned. "I imagined a foolish French doctor, a clown, you see. I thought I'd try out the character on your nurse."

"His name, his accent, everything just sprang into your mind full formed?"

"Sometimes that happens."

"Do you speak in the voices of your characters often?"

"As often as a new character arrives and demands to be . . ." For an instant he searched for the right words. "Let out."

There was something disturbing about that, something disturbing even about Will when he portrayed Dr. Caius. He truly seemed to *be* someone other than himself. Which was all right when we stood within the confines of the Rose, on the stage, where such things belonged. But here . . . I found the entire incident troubling.

I pulled the key from my pocket. Before I turned it in the lock I warned, "She may try to—" I twisted my hand, and the door erupted outward.

I landed on my arse. I expected Nurse to leap over me— she was nimble for a woman her age. She'd escape, fetch the authorities, and I might very well discover myself in Newgate, Ludgate, or behind some other "gate" by the morrow.

However, when I jumped to my feet, Will had already snatched her around the waist and hoisted her over his shoulder. He was so much stronger than he appeared.

"*Mademoiselle,*" he said. "Let me introduce *moíself.*"

Her head hung down his back, her legs kicking at his hard,

flat stomach. I forced that image from my mind lest I lose track of the issue at hand.

Then one of her knees landed on Will's nose hard enough to make it bleed—except it didn't—and he slapped her sharply on the rump. She let out a hoarse *squack* and stilled.

The sound explained why she wasn't kicking and *screaming*. She'd screamed her voice away. That also explained Jamie's report of a quiet afternoon. I should feel remorse over the loss, but I didn't. Forsooth, I couldn't help but hope it was permanent.

Will dumped Nurse unceremoniously onto the pallet in the far corner. "I am Dr. Caius," he said, "come to help you now." He waved his hand authoritatively toward the door. "Shut!" Then, when I'd complied, "Lock!"

He lowered his hand and pointed a long, slim, ink-stained finger at Nurse, who was attempting to scramble off the pallet but was hampered by her skirts, which were twisted about her legs, and the mainsail, which had tilted precariously to the side, threatening to tumble off and reveal at last the shade of her hair.

"*Asscyes-vous!*" Will ordered.

Nurse stilled. "Aye?"

"She's deaf," I said.

Will looked at me as if to say, *That too?* before he returned his attention to the old woman.

"Sit!" he roared into her ear. She fell back as if the force of his shout had a power all its own.

"Now." Will brushed his palms together. "I must examine you."

Nurse turned her attention to me, confusion washing

over her face. Then her eyes widened. "Madam!" She lifted shaking hands to her mouth and shook her head.

I glanced down; I had not changed out of my boy's clothes. God's wounds! I was an idiot!

Will flicked his fingers in that commanding yet slightly effeminate manner he'd adopted. "Do not vorry about dat. Most of de servants have fled in fear of dere lives, and de mistress has had to help in both de house and de stables."

He lied so easily and so well. I wasn't sure if I should be happy about that or concerned.

"Why have they fled?" Nurse asked.

Will laid his palm against her nose, fingers straight up as if instructing her to *halt*. Nurse's eyes crossed as she stared at his hand. "Because you have de plague."

She jerked away and promptly rapped her head against the stable wall. "I do not!"

"I am de doctor, and I say you do." He raised one long, clever finger. "Vatch dis." He waved it in front of her, back and forth like the wagging tail of a dog. Nurse's head wagged too. She winced and reached up to touch what must be a knot at the back.

Will nodded as if his fears had been confirmed. "Headache," he said. "Cold nose. Lost voice. Definitely de plague."

Nurse scowled. "I do not—"

Will lifted his finger. "You do. I am de doctor, come all de vay from Paree. I know of vat I speak." He leaned down and stared into her eyes. "*Oui?*"

Nurse's frown smoothed out. "Well, I suppose if ye came all that way." She turned her gaze to me. "Ye brought me a doctor from France, child." She clasped her bony hands to her bony bosom. "Thank ye. Everyone knows they are the most learned."

Will faced me and lifted his brows. I resisted the urge to roll my eyes. Learned indeed.

"Mayhap I do feel a bit unwell," Nurse continued.

"You must rest," Will ordered. "Lie abed. Do not attempt to leave dis room."

"Yes, Doctor," she said, as if he'd hypnotized her.

"I will tell you when it is safe to rise again. *Comprenez-vous?*"

The words must have been close enough to English for Nurse to decipher because she nodded and lay down.

Will covered her with the quilt, then patted her on the head. "You must do as I say if you wish to—"

"See the babe," she interrupted.

Will gulped. "Babe?"

Holy hell!

"*Oui!*" Nurse chirped. "The mistress is with child."

Will glanced toward me. I suddenly felt a bit ill myself.

"What was I thinking?" Nurse attempted to get up. "I cannot leave her alone when she is in such a condition." The woman's devotion was really beyond the pale.

Will pressed her back down, none too gently. "I had thought you vould be all right vith rest, but I vas mistaken. Ve must bleed you. *Oui?*"

"Bleed her?" I repeated. That seemed to be going a bit far.

Will drew his rapier. The sound it made as it slid free had the nurse turning white. When the candlelight sparked off the long, sharp edge, she fainted.

Will's lips quirked, and he sheathed his sword. "I think she'll be fine."

Chapter Twenty-six

"To mourn a mischief that is past and gone
is the next way to draw new mischief on."

—*Othello* (Act I, scene 3)

Kate was with child? Why was he surprised?

She was married; it was only a matter of time until she got with child. As much as they liked to pretend, Kate wasn't his, and she never could be.

Will snatched up the candle and followed Kate from the stables, his amusement with the character of Dr. Caius quickly fading.

"Mistress! Your bread and wine!"

The boy stood in the doorway of the house, glowering. Will couldn't blame the lad. *He'd* want to murder anyone who looked at Kate the way he did.

"In my chambers, Jamie."

The glower became a full-out snarl. But the boy did as he was told.

Will had planned to leave, but he discovered he could not. He had to hear what she would say.

As soon as Jamie set down the tray and stomped from the

room, gifting Will with a warning stare as he went, Will fell to his knees and pressed his cheek to Kate's belly. "Why didn't you tell me?"

He would have been gentler with her. Life was a gift. He knew that better than most.

"There was nothing to tell."

She'd tensed when he went to the floor, but now she relaxed, running her fingers through his hair and cupping his head to press him more firmly against her. Will stayed that way for several seconds—it felt so good to be in her embrace, he could not end it quite yet.

"There is no babe, Will."

"But your nurse—"

"Is an imbecile." Will pulled back and peered into Kate's face. She lifted a brow. "She believed what *you* told her."

Will stiffened, insulted. "I was a physician."

"You were a fool."

Well, that had been the character. But Will had thought he'd done very well, considering how little he knew of the profession.

"She assumed I was with child, and I let her so she'd leave me be." Kate lifted her chin. "And I'm *not* sorry."

"You're certain," Will began.

"I am."

"How certain?"

Kate looked away, coloring. Just so. He should not speak to her of these things. They might have shared their bodies, their hearts, their dreams and minds, but the intimate details of their daily lives—

"Very," she stated.

Will winced. Certainly he was a centuries-old necro-vampire, he'd killed his share of humans, but discuss a woman's courses, and he became as squeamish as the next man.

"Although . . ." Kate tilted her head, met his eyes, within hers a dawning concern. "Perhaps . . ."

She thought she might be with child because of him. He could not let her continue to believe that. There would never be a child with him.

"No," he said, and took her hand, pressing a kiss to her palm before continuing. "I cannot, sweet Kate."

"I think you can. Have. Will again."

He climbed to his feet. "I am incapable of fathering a child on any woman."

Kate's eyes widened. "How can you know this?"

He lied as he always did, easily and without compunction. "Because I never have."

He expected her to color at the implication of all the women he'd had, but he should have known that Kate would never behave as expected. Instead, she nodded slowly, and said, "That's good."

"Excuse me?"

"Oh!" Now she did color. "I'm sorry, Will. That was insensitive. You might want children. Why wouldn't you?"

Because he could become a blood-sucking fiend when provoked, and children were nothing if not provoking? However, he couldn't say that.

"You do not want children?" he asked. What woman did not want children?

"I like children. What I do not care for is how one gets them."

Will blinked. He'd thought she'd cared for it quite a lot.

Kate laughed. "I can read every thought in your head

upon your face, Will Shakespeare. Do not worry. Your prowess is unequaled. 'Tis *childbirth* I'd prefer to avoid. Not the child or the manner of getting one."

A shadow darkened her eyes, and her laughter died as her gaze shifted behind him.

For an instant Will believed she'd seen a zombie and glanced over his shoulder even as he reached for his sword. "What is it?"

"Nothing." She stepped forward and put her hand over his. "We are safe here."

He didn't think so. Zombies were everywhere, but her expression was such that he could not help himself; he kissed her. The embrace seemed to soothe her as nothing else would. It certainly soothed him.

"What makes your eyes so sad, sweet Kate?" he asked as she laid her head on his shoulder.

"My mother died in childbed when I was twelve. It is not a pleasant way to die, Will."

"You saw?"

"Of course. I was old enough to help."

Will had seen childbirth. It was messy, loud, downright terrifying. No child had any business watching. No wonder Kate wanted nothing to do with the process.

"My husband married me for the money my father offered, the barony Papa will buy for him once the plantation makes a profit. And my only use beyond that is as the vessel for his heir." She strode to the balcony and stared out at the moon. "It is demeaning, Will."

He'd never considered that a woman might not be happy in the role assigned to her. Stupid on his part—what human being would want to be sold and bred like a prize horse?

Take Queen Bess for example—in Will's opinion a more intelligent woman did not live and breathe on this earth. She was unmarried and would most likely stay that way until the end of her days.

Kate's discontent made Will want to catch her up in his arms, leap from the balcony, and run as far and as fast as he could to somewhere they would be safe, happy, and together. He even took one step in that direction before he remembered.

The zombies.

The necro-vampire.

The fate of London and all who lived there.

He couldn't leave, and Kate wouldn't.

So Will stood in the center of her room, the scent of her floating all around him, making him dizzy with a need to touch her. But he couldn't; he wouldn't. Right now she just needed—

"Stay," she murmured.

"Huh?"

What a gift he had with words. Such talent!

Will cleared his throat, tried to think of something brilliant to say, got nothing.

Kate turned from the window, her face exquisite with beauteous sadness.

There, that was better.

"Stay with me tonight, Will."

"I do not think—"

"Lie by my side. Make me believe there are good men in this world."

Will wasn't sure how good he was. And man? Not really. But he couldn't leave her now.

He slept!

Will could not recall the last time he'd done so in a natural, human way. When every dawn brought death, why waste time in sleep?

Even when he lay with a woman, he did not succumb to the drag and drain of exhaustion that usually followed. Nay, he would be up and writing after such an occurrence.

But lying in Kate's bed, with Kate in his arms, cuddled against his chest, he was so relaxed, the next thing he knew he heard, "Pssst!" and awoke.

A man stood in the corner.

Will glanced at Kate, but she had turned away, her dark lashes casting darker shadows upon her smooth, supple cheeks.

"Master Shakespeare!"

Will, who had been in the midst of retrieving his sword, froze. Zombies couldn't articulate. Which meant—

Not a zombie but a—

"Ghost," he muttered.

Will climbed out of bed wearing nothing but his undershirt and motioned for the man to join him on the balcony. There Will peered into the gloom. Short, swarthy, dark hair, dark eyes, weak chin, long nose, nothing about the visitor struck a chord with Will at all.

"You do not remember me, " the man said.

Italian accent. Still nothing.

"Should I?"

"You killed me in Verona."

"Sorry."

In the beginning, the bloodlust was all Will had known. As time passed, and he needed blood less and less, he'd been able to control how much he took. But before he'd gotten his mind right, he'd killed. He could not recall whom or how many.

They came to him in the night and the day; they wanted Will to tell their stories. He believed it was the least he could do.

"A gentleman of Verona," Will began.

"Two actually."

"Two?"

"You said you were famished."

Will sighed. "Where is the other?"

"He had a meeting."

Will waited for the rest of the joke, but the man wasn't laughing. Will very nearly asked about the meeting, then decided if the fellow's friend was having tea with Satan, Will really didn't want to know.

"Your name?" Will asked.

"Valentine."

That had possibilities.

"And the other?"

"Proteus. We were comrades for most of our lives. In truth, he died trying to save me. You—"

Will held up a hand. "Is this part of the story you wish me to tell?" Valentine shook his head. "Then pray move on."

Will had enough memories of horrific times past. He did not need any more.

"I went off to see the world. Paused in Milan. By the by, Proteus was sent there by his father. We fell in love with the same woman, Silvia, the daughter of a duke. However, Proteus, the knave, had already promised himself to Julia."

"And who might Julia be?"

"A lady of Verona. She disguised herself as a man to travel safely to Milan and be reunited with Proteus."

Will glanced into the room, where Kate continued to sleep. "Better and better," he murmured.

"I became an outlaw."

Will's attention snapped back to Valentine. "Really? And then?"

"Daring swordfights, kidnapping, chases, rescue."

Will nodded and stroked his beard. "All good. How does it end?"

"Well, Proteus lost his mind for a moment and tried to force Silvia."

Will growled. There was little he hated more than a man who forced himself upon women.

"But I stepped in," Valentine said hurriedly, "and since he was in such a state, offered him Silvia. However, he decided he'd rather have Julia instead."

"With friends like you two," Will muttered, "my enemies are suddenly quite appealing."

Valentine appeared confused. He obviously wasn't the brightest candle on the candle beam. Will would like to see Valentine attempt to give Kate away to her would-be rapist. There wouldn't be much left of him when she was finished.

"What's so funny, sir?" Valentine asked.

"Nothing."

"But you were chuckling."

"I do that."

Valentine still appeared confused, but he let the matter drop. "Will you write our story?"

"I believe that I will." It was perfect. A part for him, a part for Kate, even a part for Alleyn. All would be happy. "I'd like to start—"

"Will?"

Both Will and Valentine froze. Then Valentine dived headfirst over the side of the balcony. Will nearly shouted for the man to stop before he killed himself, then he remembered.

Valentine was already dead.

"She can't see you," Will muttered.

"See who?" Kate stood in the doorway. Hair tousled, long, white nightgown twisted in sleep, her feet bare . . . Will had to swallow quickly lest he drool.

"I was just—writing."

Kate looked pointedly around the balcony. No quill. No paper. Only Will.

He shrugged. "In my—" He tapped his head.

"You were talking out loud."

"Did I wake you?" He put his arm around her and led her into the room.

"Were you practicing dialogue?"

"Yes." He inched her toward the bed.

She cast him a glance. "Then why were you only doing one side of the conversation?"

Because the other side was being handled by the ghost.

Will didn't want to lie to her, but if he told her the truth, she'd cut off his head for a necro-vampire before he had a chance to explain. That would be a difficult way to start the morning. So Will did the only thing he could think of.

He kissed her.

Chapter Twenty-seven

"The devil can cite scripture for his purpose."
—*The Merchant of Venice* (Act I, scene 3)

Will was behaving strangely, which, for Will, was saying quite a bit. He was an artist, a writer of incredible gifts, but sometimes he was downright odd.

I'd heard him talking as if to someone, pausing as if to listen, then answering questions that hadn't been asked. Most wrote off his eccentricities as genius, but what if he was just insane?

I wouldn't believe that. A lunatic wouldn't kiss like an angel and make love like the devil himself.

Or at least I didn't think so.

What did I know about kisses, love, sex, genius, or even lunatics for that matter?

The familiar taste of him seduced me. Earlier, I'd only wanted Will to remain near, to show me that a man could care about me for reasons other than my body and what it could bring him.

But now. Ah, now.

I pulled him onto the bed. My hands crept beneath the linen of his shirt, my palms spreading across the smooth, cool flesh beneath. I swept my tongue along his lips, tugged the lower one into my mouth, and teased. He sighed and settled himself more firmly between my legs.

His fingers began to lift the skirt of my gown, first air on my skin, then skin on skin, gliding along the back of my knee, my thigh, then higher still. I arched at the sensation, and he cursed, stilled. His forehead touched mine, and his lips lifted, leaving me bereft.

"What's the matter?"

"The lark. I must go. 'Tis nearly morn."

I wrapped my legs around his when he would have gone away. "'Twas not the lark but the nightingale. She sings every eve on the pomegranate tree just there." I pointed to the tree, one limb visible from the bed, although upon it I saw no nightingale. "Believe me, Will, it was the nightingale."

He shook his head and disentangled himself from my embrace. "It was the lark, the herald of the morn, no nightingale." He moved to the window. "Look, love, what envious streaks do lace the severing clouds in yonder east. Night's candles are burnt out, and jocund day stands tiptoe on the misty mountain tops."

For an instant I was so enthralled by his words, I neglected to piece together their meaning. But when he began to gather his clothes, I understood rightly enough. He planned to leave while my body still cried out for his.

"That light is not daylight," I scoffed. "It is some meteor the sun exhales."

Will lifted a brow, and I drew one finger from my collarbone to my center, pausing to meander over the swell of my breasts along the way. Will gulped.

"Stay yet," I whispered. "You need not be gone."

He took one shaky step toward me, and I held out my arms. He came into them like a child to a mother he had thought lost. We tumbled to the bed, me laughing as he murmured against my breasts, "Let me be put to death. I am content. I'll say yon gray is not the morning's eye. Nor that is not the lark, whose notes do beat the vaulty heaven so high above our heads. I have more care to stay than will to go. Come, death, and welcome! Kate wills it so."

"Wait! What?" I pushed him away. "Death. What are you muttering about?"

Will blinked the hazy love-lust from his eyes. "I must—" He shook his head, and the last vestige of confusion fled. "I must meet with the backers of the Rose at dawn. They need a play from me or—"

My eyes widened. "They will *kill* you?"

He fell back upon the bed with his arm across his face. "Doubtful. But one never knows."

I glanced at the window. Was the sky actually turning gray? Yes!

"Begone. Away!" I leaped to my feet, reached down and tugged on Will with all my might. For a slight man, he was very hard to move. "It is the lark that sings so out of tune, straining harsh discords and unpleasing sharps."

Will dropped his arm and stared at me as if I was a lunatic. Maybe I was. But the idea of his being hurt or killed because I'd kept him here out of selfishness . . .

I could not bear it. And because of that, I blabbered.

"Some say the lark makes sweet division between day and night." I yanked ever harder, and at last Will lifted himself from the bed. "I will not agree to that sweetness, for she is separating us."

I bent and grabbed his clothes, tossing them at him so hard and fast his doublet hit him in the face and fell to the floor.

"Some say the lark traded eyes with the toad." Will retrieved the wrinkled doublet and slipped into it, but not before giving me a look that plainly said, *Huh?* "Now I wish they had traded voices too. The lark's voice tears us out of each other's arms."

At last he was dressed, and I shoved him none too gently toward the balcony. "Begone. More light and light it grows."

Outside in the gray haze that preceded dawn, he paused, turned, and kissed me once before vaulting over the rail and clambering down the trellis. I leaned over, afraid he'd fall, but he was nimble and all too quick.

He glanced up, and his hair blew back, the coming rays of the sun catching the pirate gold of his earring and making it sparkle. "Go to sleep, Kate. I'll see you at rehearsal."

"Maybe I should come with you. Wait right—"

"No!"

The volume of the word made me start.

He rubbed a hand over his face, then glanced at the eastern horizon. A line of orange had appeared.

"I mean, no need. I have a play." He knocked on his temple with his knuckles. "It sprang full into my head last night." He kissed his fingers, then blew the kiss to me. "Because of you, sweet Kate, my muse. *Two Gentlemen of Verona* I call it. What think you?"

"Intriguing," I said.

"Let's hope. Now go inside and shut the doors so I know you are safe."

He watched me until I did as he asked. Or he thought I had. As soon as the latch clicked, he spun and headed for the garden wall.

But as soon as it clicked, I gently opened it again so I could watch him away. I would have so few opportunities in this lifetime.

He was talking to himself again, animatedly, moving his hands, even laughing. I found myself shaking my head and smiling. He was just Will. That was what he did.

"Br—! Br—!"

The sound cut through the peaceful gray light of the coming morn. I snatched my weapon and was onto the balcony, set to vault over as he had done, in an instant. Will might be stronger than he looked, but he didn't handle a sword like I did.

As I reached the railing, I paused, sword clanking against the ground as my grasp went limp.

A large zombie—at least two heads taller than Will and probably four stone heavier—stepped from behind a tree. Without so much as a glance, Will reached out and, with his bare hands, yanked the fiend's head from his body.

As the ashes twirled like rain, Will leaped nimbly onto the garden wall, then onto the street below, and continued on his way.

Chapter Twenty-eight

"There's small choice in rotten apples."
—*The Taming of the Shrew* (Act I, scene I)

Will was sorry he'd had to lie to Kate about where he was going and why, but wouldn't it have been worse to burst into ashes in her arms?

Besides, there'd been a damn zombie in the garden. The thing could have snuck up on them while they'd been otherwise occupied. Better that he'd taken care of it before anyone was hurt.

Once over the wall, Will glanced about. Finding no one in the vicinity, he raced the sun home. Thankfully, he could run as fast as the sun if he was of a mind to—and didn't care if anyone saw him. Right now, with the horizon turning from muted orange to flames of yellow and red, he didn't care.

Will kept a room in Southwark, between the Rose and London Bridge, where he could rest in peace. He'd bought some "human" items—chairs, table, chest, bed. He even used a few of them. He kept his clothes in the chest; he had been known to leave his work upon the desk—when he wasn't

188 ✛ Lori Handeland

having trouble writing and therefore practically living in the tiring room at the Rose—but he spent most of his time out of sight.

In one wall hung a plank that appeared to be secure but wasn't. Instead, it slid easily aside so that he could slip behind and into the resting place he'd devised.

He had barely made it inside, pulled the board into place, and secured it when the sun burst free. Then, as he did every morning, Will died. He would not move, even to breathe, until that sun traveled past its apex.

For vampires, breathing was something they did to look human. Will no longer needed breath. His heart no longer beat. He was a walking corpse, just like the zombies. Maybe more so since he'd been walking much longer.

When the darkness came, often a spark of fear accompanied it. Would someone find him while he slept the sleep of the dead? Would they cut off his head? Would he never wake again? But the fear was always short-lived, drowned by that sea of black.

The dead do not dream, and Will was no different. The void he went into at dawn was just that. When he awoke it would be as if the time in between had never occurred. He'd been known to fall into his stupor halfway through a sentence and awaken to finish the thought as if he'd never been interrupted.

Will missed dreams. He'd often gotten his best ideas while asleep.

Later that day, Will awoke and set out for the Rose.

"Tell me what ye want!" *Smack!* "And quit sayin' 'br!'"

A local fruit vendor held a tall, gangly youth by his ruff.

He shook him. The youth said, "Brrrrrrr—" and reached for the man's head, teeth snapping.

Will glanced around. No one else seemed to notice, or perhaps they just didn't care.

Ah, London.

"What is wrong with ye?" The vendor tried to hold off the young man, but he was stronger. Probably had been even before he'd died.

Will stepped in. "Allow me, sirrah." Will snatched the boy and tossed him a few feet down the street. The zombie stumbled and fell.

As his knee hit the pavement, Will, with his superior hearing, detected a crunch. 'Sblood! The thing would have no choice but to shamble now.

"I will take care of this," Will told the vendor.

"What is *wrong* with him?" the man asked.

"What do you think?"

The man's eyes widened. "The plague!" He clapped his palms over his mouth, then turned and ran away.

By the time Will caught up to the zombie, the fiend had gained his feet. His left leg did not support his weight. Every time he attempted to shamble, he fell onto the ground again.

Will cursed his superior strength. He'd wanted to follow the beast back to his maker. Instead, he'd damaged him beyond repair.

The next time the zombie got up, Will caught him before he fell back down. Then he assisted him into the nearest alley. He came out dusting off his hands.

He'd just have to find another. Shouldn't be too difficult.

Will hadn't gone three dozen steps when he caught sight of a figure heading in the opposite direction as fast as it could. People on the street gave him a wide berth. He did appear to have, if not the plague, then something just as bad.

Will kept his distance, scuttling from doorway to doorway, as the zombie made his way out of town.

London is a big city, one of the largest in Europe, and, when in the midst of it, Will always felt overwhelmed. Which was probably why he often forgot that the countryside could be encountered by walking in any direction.

Certainly, London was bordered on three sides by the city walls and the fourth by the Thames; however, the town had spread past the walls in several places, and if you walked far enough, the countryside would just appear—surprise!—on the other side of the street.

Which was exactly what happened to Will. He stopped at a corner, pulling back when the zombie glanced over his shoulder. When Will looked again he was gone.

Thinking that the fiend had headed past the buildings, Will hurried after, but when he reached the end of the street, Will stared into a great vast emptiness.

Trees and fields and grass but no zombie.

"Fie," Will muttered. "A pox upon you."

Not that the pox would do the risen dead any harm, but that was beside the point.

Will saw no place where the fiend could easily hide. And why would he hide? Even if he'd seen Will following him, he would have been more likely to change direction and come after Will in hopes of a brain breakfast.

So . . .

Will's gaze wandered over the houses stacked so closely together on both sides of the street that their roofs seemed to meet in the middle and block out the afternoon sun. There had to be a dozen homes. He was going to have to check each and every one. Will put his hand on his sword and began to knock on doors.

Will had an affinity for the dead. He would know at first glance if the raiser of zombies opened the door. He would recognize a like being instantly. Then one slice and this would all be over. Will could go back to writing his new play, and Kate would never have to learn the truth.

He should have known nothing was ever that simple.

The first house was quite obviously that of a family. The wife answered his knock; she had several urchins clinging to her skirts. She nearly grabbed his sword and skewered him with it when he said, "Sorry, wrong house."

The slam of the door made him wince. But Will wasn't deterred. He knocked on the next door and the next. No one answered either knock, so he let himself inside. He searched the premises, found no one.

Alive or dead.

At the fourth abode he was successful, though not in the way he'd hoped.

A heavy woman with a dirty apron and a dirtier face opened the door. Her dour expression had Will backing away lest she smack him across the mouth with the dead chicken she appeared to be plucking. However, the scowl turned upside down at the sight of him.

"Will Shakespeare?" she asked. "'Tis really you?"

She moved closer, the scent of her making Will take another step back. He nearly stumbled over his own feet and fell into the muck of the street.

"Are we acquainted, madam?"

This was what happened when you lived forever. Everyone began to look alike.

"No, sir. I saw you perform at the Rose time and again. I'm your biggest follower."

Will eyed her extremely large girth, which she'd had to turn sideways to fit through the door, and decided she was most likely right.

"Oh," Will said. "How . . . lovely."

The woman began to stalk him. One step forward for her, two steps back for him. The skirt of her rough wool gown swayed. He didn't care for the expression in her eyes. She appeared hungrier than a starving vampire.

"I have always wanted to meet ye."

"And now you have. But I'm afraid I must be—"

She dropped the chicken to the ground and snatched Will's hand. "Oh, Master Shakespeare, I've written a play."

"Urgh," was all he could manage as she squeezed his fingers in the maw of her huge, damp hands. Chicken feathers clung here and there; others drifted away upon the wind.

"It is only a few scenes long, but I think most plays drone on. And the story is perhaps not the fashion, but that won't matter once you read it. 'Tis brilliant. Much better even than anything *you've* done. I know you'll want to perform it at the Rose directly." She let him go and clasped her hands beneath her chins. "Then I will be rich for all of my days."

A stray feather tickled her nose, and she sneezed, once, twice, three times, all over her hands and all over Will.

"That is—uh—very talented of you, madam."

Most women of her class couldn't read, let alone write. He wondered what was the matter with this one.

Perhaps she saw the question on his face. Regardless, she answered it. "My father was a clergyman and I his only child. On long winter nights he taught me all that he knew."

"Good of him," Will said. What he thought was: *Why, then, are you here?*

But that would have been a foolish question. The woman might be able to read and write, but what good would it do her in a world ruled by men. Queen Bess was the exception, not the rule. Even Kate lived a life she did not wish for.

The woman turned back toward her home. "I'll get you the pages. Tomorrow I will come to the Rose. You can tell me how much you will pay."

She disappeared through the door. Will stood there for several seconds, amazed at the height and breadth of her delusion. First, that he would ever read her story. He had enough of his own battering at his head.

Second, that he would have the thing read by the morrow if he read it at all. He was good but not that good.

Third, that she would be paid before someone funded the play, and that she would get rich from it.

Will decided he could return and search for zombies on a different day, or perhaps find another zombie and go somewhere else entirely. He liked the latter idea better.

Will turned away from his biggest follower's door and ran.

Straight into a zombie. Why were they always around when you didn't want them to be, yet there was never one to be had when you were looking?

Will bounced off the man's wide chest and nearly fell to the ground. His graceless movement caused the fiend's grasping arms to meet pure air. Will gained his feet and sped away.

"Wait!"

Will couldn't help it. He glanced back. The woman lumbered after him, waving a handful of papers. "You forgot this."

Will didn't pause.

Until she screamed.

Chapter Twenty-nine

"These words are razors to my wounded heart."
—*Titus Andronicus* (Act I, scene I)

I sank to my knees on the morning-cool floor of my balcony. Will Shakespeare wasn't human. No one could be human and do something like that.

It was as if the film over my eyes had been lifted. I didn't much like the view.

Me in the dark alley, rapier in hand, having just killed the tibonage. Someone touches me and I spin, slicing Will's neck from ear to ear. Him falling, the shower of blood a fountain. Then later, Will miraculously alive with nary a scratch.

Human? I didn't think so.

Master Shakespeare, a poet, yet so quick and strong. Lean and lanky, true, but the muscles beneath his smooth, luscious skin were as hard as if he'd been hauling rocks from a field for decades. Did Christopher Marlowe possess such strength? Doubtful.

Another image came to mind. Will going over my balcony rail and appearing on the ground before I managed to look over the edge. Such speed was suspect, yet never had

I suspected. I was too enthralled with the man and the music of his words.

The longer I pondered, the more questions poured into my head.

Had I ever seen Will stand beneath the sun?

No.

"Meeting at dawn, my arse," I muttered. "Mayhap the dawn will set you aflame."

Right now, *I* wanted to.

He'd yanked that zombie's head completely free from the body without a backward glance, then leaped *onto* my garden wall.

"And I heard you were once a schoolmaster." I made a tsking sound. He behaved unlike any schoolmaster I'd ever known.

He was something, I thought, but what? I knew so little about anything but zombies, and he wasn't that. However, I had learned a bit lately about the being that could raise them.

"Affinity for the dead," I murmured, and my skin prickled.

Zombies constantly turned up wherever we were. I'd thought it because there were so damn many of them, we couldn't help but stumble over a few. Now I had to wonder if they'd been drawn to Will like—

"Ghosts."

The memory of him talking to himself on this very balcony only an hour before assaulted me. Did he speak to characters from his imagination? Or spirits only he could see?

If Will was a necromancer, a vampire, that would explain a lot of things.

Including the zombie army.

Chapter Thirty

"Out of the jaws of death."

—*Twelfth Night* (Act III, scene 4)

Will looked back, but it was already too late to help the woman. Zombies poured from the houses. At first they took no notice of her, intent on chasing him.

But as she began to claw at them, smacking a few on the head with her manuscript, trying to make her way to the front of the pack, they turned on her.

Will didn't see what happened—praise the saints. But from her screams, nothing good, and he couldn't wait around.

The zombies were after him.

What he couldn't figure out was why. He'd done nothing to harm them. He hadn't had time.

"Be careful!"

Will had no idea who shouted, but he turned his head and narrowly missed going arse over tip. A zombie stood directly in his path.

Will leaped, straight up and over, leg outstretched as if he'd like to kick someone in the face. He would, but there was no one there. As of now they were all behind him.

A pack of shamblers was no match for Will Shakespeare. He was long away before they even reached the outskirts of London. Not that they couldn't find him. The damned fiends always found him.

And why was that?

Certainly, he had an affinity for the dead, but he'd never had this many encounters with them before in any lifetime. There had to be a reason for it.

Will took a circuitous route until he was certain no one had followed. When at last he reached the Rose and ducked inside, the place was bustling. For an instant he just stood and let the scent, the sight, the sound of this place he loved so much wash over him.

Henslowe had taken care to build the Rose solidly, upon a firm, brick foundation. The beams were timber, the walls lath and plaster. Three levels it comprised, the least-expensive seats on the ground, the best higher up.

Like most theaters, the Rose contained an upper level behind the stage so playwrights could add directions such as *from above*. If Will wished, he could portray heaven and earth, as well as hell, since there was trapdoor in the stage through which players could appear and disappear.

Will called for silence, and all eyes turned to him. "Tonight we will begin to rehearse a new play."

Cheers, whistles, applause met this announcement before the bustle began again. Will smiled. There was something special about a new play.

He'd best get to writing it.

Entering the tiring room, Will tried to calm himself with deep, steady breaths. He'd begun to pant sharply while running, though he really didn't need to. He just got so used to behaving like a human.

"Dat was very close."

Will yelped and spun about. The dark-skinned woman in the brightly colored clothes and turban was back. But this time he had a pretty good idea who she was. African accent, French words, Moorish complexion, 'twasn't hard.

"Nounou, I presume?"

She smiled, bright teeth flashing, before she lowered her chin in acknowledgment.

"If I'd fallen before that zombie horde, no telling what might have happened." He swept a bow. "Thank you for calling out."

"'Twas de least I could do. You have made my girl so happy."

"She's made me happy. I love her."

"And she loves you." Nounou frowned. "Or she did."

Will, who'd felt like he wanted to fly at her first words, suddenly felt like he wanted to die at her second. "Wh-what?" he stuttered. "Why?"

The old woman's wise, dark gaze met his. "She suspects what you are."

"How could she?"

"She saw you in the garden."

For an instant Will had no idea what Nounou meant. He barely remembered leaving Kate that morning. He'd been speaking with Valentine, thinking about the new play, working out the plot and the characters, and then—

Something had happened. Will squinted, trying to recall.

Br—!

Hell! She'd seen him tear the head off that zombie like a mad beast.

Nounou watched the understanding pass over his face and nodded. "You must make certain you convince her udderwise."

"How?"

She spread her long-fingered, graceful hands. "Lie."

Will sighed. "That shouldn't be too hard."

"If she suspects you are not human, she will never trust you. She will waste time hunting you. Most importantly, she will never hunt *wit'* you, and she must."

"Again I ask, 'why?'"

"You know dere are too many of dem. She needs help, and you will let no harm befall her while you are dere."

Will would die a thousand deaths beneath the morning sun before he let anyone or anything hurt Kate. However—

"What if I told her the truth?"

"No!" Nounou exclaimed.

"But if she understood that with her skill and my strength, we could not be defeated . . ." Nounou was shaking her head, and Will's voice trailed off.

"I made a mistake," Nounou murmured. "I did not know dere were some of your kind who were not murdering fiends. I taught her to kill anyt'ing dat wasn't human."

"But what if I—?"

"She'll believe no one but me."

"I could tell her that you—"

"The instant you tell her you've spoken to me, you are doomed. Only a necromancer can speak to de dead."

Will drew himself up. "You think she could kill me?"

"I *know* dat she could."

Will knew she could too. And while he'd gladly give up his life to save her, he wasn't willing to give it up *to* her. He would not allow Kate to face the army of zombies and an unknown necro-vampire alone.

Because *that* she would not survive.

Chapter Thirty-one

"Et tu, Brute!"
—*Julius Caesar* (Act III, scene 1)

I did not reach the Rose until long after noon. I'd wanted to leave right away, to be there before Will arrived. However, I had Nurse to deal with.

I'd given orders that no one take care of her but me. Which meant I actually had to do so.

Thankfully, she had accepted Will's impersonation of Dr. Caius completely. When I opened the door to the stable room, Nurse lay on the bed moaning. Since there was nothing wrong with her, I had to grit my teeth to keep from telling her so.

"Good nurse," I began.

"Ay, me!" she shouted, grabbing at her mainsail kerchief, which she still wore despite lying abed since yesterday. "My aching head. Pray be more quiet, child."

I opened my mouth to point out that she was the one who was shouting, then snapped it closed again. She wouldn't hear me. Because she never stopped talking.

"I had the chills, a fever it was. I called for help, but no one came."

"I'm he—"

"Then dreams I had. So horrible. Of fire and flames, like hell it seemed."

"That's what spying will get you," I muttered as I brought in her food and drink.

"Aye?" Nurse cupped her ear. "What say you?"

"You must keep up your strength!" I shouted.

She winced. "My head! Pray be silent."

I needed to leave before I silenced *her*. "I will return later." Much, *much* later.

Nurse grabbed my hand. "Could you sit, child? Keep me company whilst I eat? Perhaps read to me? I ache with the fever."

"You can't hear," I pointed out.

"Eh?" She cupped her ear.

In the end, I sat with her while she ate—the "fever" hadn't tempered her appetite—then read from a religious pamphlet I found in a corner of the stable. Mayhap she could hear the rhythm of the words, because she dozed off.

By the time I'd spoken to Cook, then instructed Jamie to deal with the horses as he saw fit—he knew more about them than I did—I could easily escape to my room for an afternoon "nap." I left strict orders not to be disturbed.

In moments I had dressed as Clayton and climbed down the trellis to the garden. Since the gardener had fled with the rest of my servants, I had no concern that anyone would see.

The Rose was bustling; I wasn't sure why. I grabbed Edmond as he hurried past. "What has happened?"

"Did you not hear?" He clasped his fat hands beneath his

fat face in a gesture very reminiscent of Nurse, except for the fat. "Master Shakespeare has begun a new play. You will rehearse Act I this eve."

"How would I have heard that?" I asked.

"I sent a messenger to everyone's home."

"You know where I live?"

"No," Edmond said, and hurried off. I stared after him, uncertain what had just happened.

Excitement trickled through me at the thought of a new play by William Shakespeare, and I would be a part of it.

Then I remembered. I'd come here to kill him. I'd best be about my business.

As Will must be writing Act I, I assumed he was at work in the tiring room, a place he appeared to have appropriated for himself. Where the other players changed clothes, I couldn't say. Perhaps in the storage area known as "the hut," which took up the second-floor space directly above.

I opened the door and discovered my assumption correct. Bent over his desk, Will scribbled and muttered, muttered and scribbled. He had ink all over his fingers and a bit on the end of his nose. Just looking at him, my heart stuttered, then began to beat ever faster.

Such beauty. Such genius. Such a shame all that would be lost.

Oh well. *He* was the murderous, zombie-raising fiend. Not me.

I had begun to move forward, hand upon my rapier, intent on getting this over with before I changed my mind, when he spoke. "Sweet love!"

I froze. Had he seen me? Sensed me? Would he kill me now before I could kill him?

"Sweet lines! Sweet life!" he continued. "Here is her hand, the agent of her heart; here is her oath for love, her honor's pawn."

The play. It would not hurt for me to listen awhile. But his words as beautiful as his voice, those eyes and lips—I was soon lost.

"O, that our fathers would applaud our loves, to seal our happiness with their consents! O heavenly Julia!"

Julia? Who in hell is Julia? My hand went back to my sword.

Will turned his attention to a corner of the room and appeared to be listening to someone.

Except no one was there.

He nodded, once, twice, then scribbled for several minutes before pausing, cursing, and getting to his feet. He clapped his hands thrice, kicked his chair, stated firmly, "Hey, nonny, no," crossed himself, and sat down.

"What think you of this, Proteus?" he asked.

And who in hell is Proteus?

I forgot the question in the beauty of Will's next words.

"Thus have I shunn'd the fire for fear of burning, and drench'd me in the sea, where I am drown'd. I fear'd to show my father Julia's letter."

Julia again. Grrr.

"O, how this spring of love resembleth the uncertain glory of an April day, which now shows all the beauty of the sun, and by and by a cloud takes all away."

The sun! Zounds! Why hadn't I thought of that? I wouldn't have to decapitate him after all.

Will had just begun his ritual when, right between clapping his hands and kicking his chair, I stepped from the shadows.

He stilled, blinking at me owlishly as if he'd just woken from a long, pleasant nap. "Julia?" he murmured.

I fought the urge to draw my sword and whack the name Julia from his lips. "It is Kate."

A smile erupted. "Kate. I'm so glad you're here. Come and look at the play. I have the perfect part for you."

He held out his hand and, without thought, I took it. His fingers were so cold I gasped and pulled away.

"Too chill?" He rubbed them together briskly, blew on the tips several times. "My hands are forever so if I've worked them too long." He held one out again. "Come."

I braced myself—his cool skin had never bothered me before. In truth, I'd relished it—and clasped my palm to his. 'Twas better, though not warm.

Instead of following as he tried to lead me to the table, I tugged in the other direction. "Come with me."

He came without question, without qualm. How could he be so trusting of his doom?

Outside, the sun shone well enough through the clouds. I stepped into it, but he hung back, his hand in the dark, mine in the light. "What's the matter, Will?"

He glanced into the shadows of the Rose. "I need to work, Kate. We rehearse in three hours."

"Just a moment. You must see." I pointed upward and away at something just out of his range. Bracing my feet, I prepared to pull him to everlasting death if I must.

Will sighed, then stepped into the light.

I dropped his hand, lifted my own to shield my face, waited for the whoosh of flame, the flutter of ashes. I'm not ashamed to say my eyes watered. I couldn't stop them.

"Kate?" Will asked.

I dropped my arm. Not a mark on him.

He tilted his head, and his golden earring caught the sun's glare, sparking into my eyes, making them water all the more. "What did you want to show me?"

"The—uh—bird." I pointed in the same general area I'd pointed before. "'Tis—uh—gone."

He stared at me for several seconds as if he knew what I was about and found me beyond amusing. Perhaps he did. If he was the creature I believed him to be, none of what had passed between us had been real. He'd been playing with me all along.

Furious, I strode forward and yanked the neckerchief from about his neck. "Aha!" I announced, and cracked the cloth like a whip for emphasis.

Then I stared, dumbfounded, at the thin, red scar that marred his neck. Why hadn't I seen it when we'd been naked in each other's arms? My only excuse was that I'd been more interested in parts farther south.

Will took the kerchief from my limp hand and draped it around his neck once more. "Aha, what, Kate? You gave me that scar."

"I'm sorry," I whispered.

"Accidents happen." He shrugged. "Mistakes are made."

Had I made one with him? I still wasn't sure.

Chapter Thirty-two

"Do you think I am easier to be played on than a pipe?"
—*Hamlet* (Act III, scene 2)

Kate swayed, and Will caught her up in his arms, then strode toward the tiring room.

"I'm not what you think I am," Will said softly.

Her eyes widened, and she began to struggle. But he was stronger. He would never let her get away.

"Kate!" He shook her just a little. "I would not hurt you."

Several of the crew saw them coming, turned on their heels, and went the other way. Will stepped inside and kicked shut the door. Then he set her on her feet and tried not to be crushed when she scrambled behind the bench upon which they'd once made love.

"I would *never* hurt you," he said. "Even if I *were* a necro-vampire."

"How—?" She paused, swallowed, tried again. "How did you know what I was doing?"

He laughed. "I'm the one who told you how to kill them. Did you think I wouldn't recall the conversation?" He lowered his voice. "I recall every word that we have said to each other." Someday, when she found out the truth, those words and his memories would be all he had left of her.

"I saw you speaking to ghosts," she said quietly.

His gaze flicked to hers. "What ghosts?"

She waved a slim hand at the corner where Proteus had so recently stood. At least the man had gone. Will was not in the mood to have this conversation with anyone watching, even a spirit.

"You speak to empty corners. You answer questions no one else hears. You read your work as if *to* someone and await his response."

"Ah," Will said. "'Tis true I hear voices. I've been told most writers do."

"Mayhap the lunatics in Bedlam are merely writers who cannot write," she snapped.

"Mayhap," Will agreed. "If I could not write, I know I would be lost."

Her forehead creased. "Why do the tibonage follow you?"

"I thought we were following them."

Kate shook her head. "They seem to appear wherever you are."

"Do they?" Will murmured. "I hadn't noticed."

She went silent again, hand still on her sword. If she chose to cleave his head from his shoulders, she would have her truth before his ashes fluttered to her feet. But Will couldn't allow that to happen. He must protect her from the zombie plague. No one else could.

"Kate," he said quietly, "if I were raising zombies, then why on earth would I help you kill them?"

The words rang true because true they were. Will might

be a necro-vampire, but he had not raised a zombie in a very long time.

"Mmm," she murmured, though she appeared unconvinced. "There is one more thing that disturbs me. One more incident that I cannot explain away no matter how hard I try."

Uh-oh, Will thought.

"The tibonage in the garden this morning. You tore off his head, Will." Her fingers tightened around the hilt of her sword. "No human could do that."

The lie tripped easily off his tongue. "They could if the zombie was so old and decayed his head was practically lolling off his neck already."

Kate frowned. "I've never seen one like that."

"Then you are blessed, sweet Kate. It is not a pretty sight."

Will held his breath—not a difficult task considering—as Kate mulled over all he'd said, all she'd done. At last she let her hand drop from her sword, and Will made sure to take a loud, humanlike breath.

He'd convinced her. Or at least given her enough doubt that she would not cleave his head from his shoulders.

Yet.

"Come, Kate, step out from behind that bench. I would never hurt you. This you must know. Don't you feel it in your heart? If not, then I have been remiss."

Slowly she inched from behind the furniture.

"Sit," he urged.

"No." She glanced at the closed door. "You must work."

"By and by," he agreed. "But first there is something I need tell you."

Her eyebrows arched; her fingers twitched toward the

sword again, and his chest ached where his silent heart lay. Would she ever trust him completely?

"I followed a zombie toward London Bridge. There he disappeared into a home." Will quickly told her the rest of the afternoon's activities.

"They chased you?" she asked. "Yet you hadn't threatened them in any way?"

"I hadn't even discovered where they were hiding. They poured out of the buildings as if—" He paused, not wanting to add to her distrust of him. But Kate was too smart by half, and she knew what he did not say.

"As if you'd called them."

"They did," he agreed.

"And the woman who tried to stop them, they . . ." She swallowed thickly.

"Yes." Best not to describe that incident further. He could still hear the screams.

"You know what that means?" Kate asked.

"Her husband is still waiting for his dinner?"

"Will!"

"Pardon me." Sometimes the only way to keep his sanity through centuries of un-life was to poke fun at death. Will knew he should not, but sometimes he couldn't help himself.

"If you didn't threaten the zombies, yet they chased you with every intention of attacking you," she murmured, "that means their orders were—"

"To attack me."

Why hadn't he thought of that? The damn things were always underfoot. He'd never considered that they might have been ordered to be.

"But why?" Kate wondered. "The fiend would be better served to send them after me."

"No!" Will blurted, alarm causing him to shout.

"Calm down," she said. "The only reason the necro-vampire would have for sending his zombies to kill you would be to stop you from obliterating his army."

Not really, Will thought. The necro-vampire might be another playwright, although raising a zombie army was a bit much just to keep Will from writing.

However, what if he knew that Will was a necro-vampire too? Perhaps he wanted to be the only fiend in town capable of raising a zombie army. Small supply and large demand meant more money. Will knew that from experience.

"But considering that I'm the chasseur," Kate continued, "why send them after you?"

"Perhaps he does not know about you yet. Perhaps he only knows about me."

Kate snorted. "He'd have to be a fool to believe an untrained sword could turn so many of the tibonage to ashes."

"Mayhap he is a fool," Will said. But he didn't think so. He thought the necro-vampire was quite clever.

He only wished he knew what the fiend was being clever about.

Chapter Thirty-three

"Fair is foul, and foul is fair."

—*Macbeth* (Act I, scene 1)

"We'll decipher none of this today," Will said. "And I must work."

"Yes." I stepped toward the door. "I'll . . ." I paused. What would I do? It wouldn't be worth the time to walk home. I had to be back at the Rose in a few hours.

"Help with the scenery?" Will murmured as he inked his quill.

"Certainly," I agreed, and opened the door.

Will cursed, and I turned just as he clapped and kicked his chair. "What are you doing?" I asked.

He froze, face blank as if he had no idea what I was talking about.

"This," I said, then clapped thrice and kicked the wall.

"Oh." Will lifted one shoulder, a sheepish expression crossing his handsome face. "I do not even realize I'm doing it anymore."

"Doing *what*?" I reiterated patiently.

"My ritual. I perform it every time I begin to work. I'm

not sure why, but"—he waved the hand that held the quill, and a drop of ink flew—"it helps me to begin. And if the words cease to come, performing the ritual again can make them flow."

"How . . . interesting," I said.

Will's lips curved. "You'll find actors and writers a superstitious lot. Every writer I know has a ritual. Some must have ale or wine. Not English swill but French!"

His smile became a full-blown grin on the last word, and I found myself grinning back at the memory of silly Dr. Caius.

"With others, it is whiskey or water."

I made a face. No one drank water unless he *wanted* to be ill.

"They place it just so—" He patted the right corner of his table. "Or so." He patted the left. "For some their desk must be neat, for others chaotic. They wear their lucky shirts or no shirts at all. And that's just the *writers* I know. We'd be here for days if I began to list all the superstitions of the actors."

"How did you ever come up with such a complicated ritual?" I asked.

"Kate," he answered, "I have no idea."

I left Will clapping and kicking his chair. As I pulled shut the door, I heard, "Hey, nonny, no," then his arse hit the seat with a dull thump. The scratch of a quill soon followed.

Ritual. Superstition. Magic. Insanity. You needed a good dose of each to create something from nothing.

Where *did* the words come from? No one seemed to know.

I made my way to the stage, intent on helping wherever I might be needed. In my wake trailed whispers. I couldn't blame them. I *was* swiving the boss.

Well, not *the* boss, I corrected as Ned Alleyn appeared.

When we'd first been married, Reginald had tried at times to please me and had taken me to see Ned perform as Barabas in Marlowe's *The Jew of Malta.* He had been brilliant, and I had enjoyed myself immensely. Afterward, Reginald insisted I meet the man.

I'd also met Ned a few days past, though he hadn't even looked at me when he'd hired me to replace Thaddeus on the stage.

I doubted he would recognize me as a woman beneath the guise of Clayton, boy actor; nevertheless, I held my breath and willed my heart to cease thundering as the tall, handsome actor strode near.

"And who are you, boy?" he asked, his voice so deep, so strong, it seemed to carry throughout the entire theater.

Not *seemed.* Did. For the snickers that followed his question assured me that all in the building had heard.

Ned frowned. "Prithee, what is so funny?"

"I do not know, sir." I bowed. "I am Clayton. You hired me to replace one of the actors who was no longer with you."

"I did?"

"Yes, sir." I guess I didn't need to worry about him recognizing me as Kate when he didn't even recall Clayton.

"Are you any good?" he asked.

"Oh, he's good all right," someone shouted from the wings. More laughter ensued.

I knew what they were insinuating, and my face flamed. I ducked, but not before Alleyn saw. "Oh," he said, and in that comment lay a world of understanding. "I did not recognize you at first."

I kept my head down, unable to speak.

"I'd thought those rumors about Will just bad faith." He clapped me on the back so hard I stumbled forward. "No matter. I have decided that I employ him for his brains and not his rod. He may stick it wherever he likes."

"I—uh, well, good of you, sir." I was so flummoxed I dipped a curtsy, which I changed to a fumbling, hasty bow.

Alleyn frowned. "I hope you aren't this clumsy on the stage."

"No, sir. Never, sir."

"See that you aren't," he said, and walked away shouting, "Come out here, Shakespeare! Show me what you've got."

I hurried after him. "Sir! Sir!" But he paid me no mind, opening the door to the tiring room and barging within.

"What wonderful lead have you written for me this time, Will?"

I crept closer, then unabashedly hovered just outside to watch and listen in.

Will squinted into Ned's face as if he did not recognize the man. He'd covered several pages with scribbles. I guess his ritual really did work.

"William?" Alleyn snapped his fingers in front of Will's nose. "You swore you would have a new play today. Tell me of it."

"Two gentlemen," Will blurted. "Of Verona."

"Good," Ned said. "Everyone is fascinated with Italy these days. Italian rapiers carried by every man in London." He shook his head and *tsked*. "Who gets to kiss the girl?"

"Well, there are two."

"Girls?"

"And gentlemen."

"Right," Ned agreed. "Just so. And which one am I?"

"Valentine loves Silvia and—"

"Valentine. Yes. That *is* I."

"No. It is I."

"I like the name Valentine, and Silvia too for that matter. I will take that part."

"But, Ned, Proteus—"

Ned waved his hand. "You will portray him." He turned away. Will grabbed his wrist, and Ned froze.

My gaze flew to where Will's fingers grasped, just above Ned's hand. He held him; that was all. Nothing appeared amiss.

"I will be Valentine," Will said. "You will be Proteus. Proteus is the better part."

"Well," Ned said, staring into Will's dark eyes, "in that case, I will be Proteus."

Will let him go, and Ned shook his head and his hand as if both had fallen asleep.

"I'll be done with the first scene in an hour, Ned. Make sure I'm not disturbed."

"Anything you say, Will."

Ned stepped into the hall, shut the door, then stood with his arms across his chest in front of it. He glanced at me. "Go," he ordered.

I went.

But not before I looked back at Ned Alleyn standing in front of the tiring room just as he'd been ordered.

Something wasn't quite right.

Chapter Thirty-four

"My heart is true as steel."

—*A Midsummer Night's Dream* (Act II, scene 1)

The rehearsal for Act I, scene I, had gone better than Will had hoped. The parts seemed written for the actors who portrayed them.

Perhaps because they had been.

Ned made the perfect Proteus, Kate an exquisite Silvia, while Will relished the role of Valentine. First love, forever love. That was what he felt for Kate and what he poured into the play and his character. Even Ned had to admit that Will had been right to insist on the casting that he had.

And he hadn't even needed to "push" the man that time.

Will hated to exert his power over people, but sometimes he just had to.

"Come along!" Ned announced. "We're to the George."

The George, originally known as the George and Dragon, named after the legend of Saint George, was a nearby inn. The place was a stop on the coach line and also served as a playhouse in the summer. Before the Rose, Will's plays had often found an audience in the courtyard.

Though Will needed to work the whole night through—there'd be rehearsal tomorrow, and he had yet to write scene 2—once Will caught sight of Kate's face, he could not refuse. She wanted to go.

"Let us away," he called, and her smile was worth a thousand agonies.

"I've never been to a public house," she whispered as they followed the others onto the street.

The excitement in her voice was contagious. Will's step became more buoyant just listening to her.

Gently bred young ladies did not frequent Southwark inns. Certainly, if Kate had been on a trip, she might have made a stop there, partaken of a hearty mutton-and-onion stew, brown bread, a bit of cheese, and ale. However, she would have been well chaperoned, and she would not have experienced the true nature of the George from behind the doors of rooms reserved for the coach passengers. The roughness of the inn-yard and the pub were beyond her ken.

And the George was rough. They could hear the revelry before they even turned into the courtyard that bordered the entrance. Once there, the rest of the company dissolved into the crowd in an instant, leaving Will and Kate alone.

Will had to resist the urge to pull her close and keep her safe. Certainly, she appeared small and frail compared to the large, coarse patrons of the George. But the sword at her side was not for show, and Kate could take care of herself. Will didn't need to invite an argument by touching what everyone would assume to be a young boy in a manner many would find offensive.

Kit Marlowe might do it, but, then, he was Kit Marlowe.

Instead, Will ordered two pints and muscled his way to a table in the back, where they could observe apart from the milling throng.

Kate lifted her glass and took a hearty sip, then sprayed the ale all over the table when she choked. Will laughed, along with everyone else who was near, and slapped her on the back until she stopped coughing.

"Not what you're used to?" he murmured.

She merely glared at him through watering ebony eyes.

"Hey, Will, the new boy needs a set of balls," someone shouted.

Will continued to hold Kate's gaze. "What he has is quite enough," he answered, and she managed a smile.

Lifting his glass, Will tilted it toward her. "To the play," he announced.

Several of the company's members hoisted their drinks and responded, "The play!"

Kate lifted her glass, but she couldn't keep the grimace from her face as the brew came nearer and nearer to her mouth.

"Slowly," Will advised. "It isn't so bad if you take small amounts."

She nodded and did as he advised, then set the glass down with a sharp *click*.

"Better?" he asked.

"No," she responded, voice hoarse.

"You do not have to finish."

"And let them call me a *woman*?" She took a healthy swig. Her face turned red, but she swallowed, and she kept it down.

Those who had mocked her now cheered. Kate hoisted

her ale and drank. This time her face merely turned the shade of a newly plucked peach.

The glass thudded against the table. "'Tis not so bad," she said, and her smile was a bit silly.

"You're getting drunk." Will pulled the glass away.

She slapped his hand and took it back. "Something else I've never done."

"Kate," he said.

"Clay," she corrected.

"What if you must use your sword later?"

Will cursed when her joyous expression melted into one of resignation. She pushed the glass in his direction and sighed. "You're right."

"Someday when the—" He looked around. No one seemed to be paying them any mind, but there were too many people far too near to use the word *zombie*. "You know," he said. "When *they* are gone, I will take you to a pub and allow you to get royally fuddled."

"You're so good to me," she muttered.

They sat in companionable silence, neither of them drinking as the revelry moved all around them. It was only by chance that Will heard the man speak.

Chance and his superb vampire senses.

"I tell you, it was he!" The tension in the words caused them to rise above all the others.

"Ye are a fool. A drunken fool."

"I have had nothing to drink as of yet, and certainly nothing when, on my way here, I saw the murdering traitor."

Will straightened, glancing about the crowded public house.

"What?" Kate asked.

He held up a hand, and she hushed.

"He bumped into me," the man continued. "I saw his face. Closer even than when he was hanged. Then I stood directly in front of the gallows. I will not forget his likeness until I am as dead as he should be." The fellow lifted his shoulders, hunched his back, and shuddered. "The Queen ordered he be left to hang for days. His face turned black; his tongue swelled up. The birds began to pick at his eyes. 'Twas awful to see."

"And the sight must have driven ye mad. Men who are executed do not walk the streets of Southwark."

The traditional means of execution for high treason was to be hanged, drawn, and quartered, a disgusting practice where the culprit was first hanged, then taken down while still alive and made to watch his intestines being drawn out and burned, along with his genitalia. Last, but not least, the victim was sliced into four parts—quartered—then beheaded.

And they called vampires fiends.

However, after the Babington plot, when the Queen had ordered those who conspired to murder her and replace her on the throne with her cousin, Mary, Queen of Scots, executed in just this way, she'd lost the stomach for it. The description of how horrifically the first seven conspirators had died caused her to commute the sentence of the rest to hanging. As far as Will knew, she hadn't ordered the traditional punishment since.

"Damn," Will muttered. "A nice beheading fixes everything."

"What?" Kate asked, but Will again shushed her.

"I know what I saw," the first man insisted. "I must tell the authorities. God save the Queen!" he shouted.

Everyone in the George lifted their glasses and responded, "The Queen!" before returning to their conversations.

"Ye can't go about telling folks ye saw a dead man walking. Next thing ye know ye'll be drinkin' water in Bedlam instead of good English ale at the George. Have some sense, man!"

"I cannot sit here whilst such a being walks the streets of London plotting to kill Her Majesty! I won't."

The scrape of a chair was succeeded by footsteps. Will followed, Kate at his heels. He ignored the shouts urging him to join this group or that, buy a round, drink it. Nodding and waving, he continued on his way, bursting into the courtyard on the heels of their quarry.

"Sirrah?" Will called, and he turned. "I heard you speak inside about a man who should be dead but is not."

Will ignored Kate's sharply indrawn breath and gave the fellow a little "push." "Tell me about him."

He repeated all Will had already heard and then some.

"Hold." Will lifted his hand in the middle of that tale. "Execution for treason, you say?"

"I heard he was sent by Philip of Spain to kill the Queen."

Will had been too concerned of late with losing his ability to write. He'd thought of little else and paid no attention to current events. He knew nothing of this.

There were always rumors of plots to murder Elizabeth—religion, politics, foreign affairs—the world was not safe for one such as she. But often they were merely that. Rumors. Obviously, if someone had been hanged and left to rot this plot was real. And if the culprit was once again alive, so was the threat to the Queen.

"What does he look like?" Will demanded.

"Very tall and dark. Thin. Black beard with some gray. Heavy eyebrows." He glanced at Kate. "Skin as dark as his."

Kate's eyes narrowed. It *had* been rude to mention that.

"Where did you see him?"

"Headed toward London Bridge."

"You are certain it was the same fellow who was executed for treason once already?"

"Yes, your worship. I would know Guy de Nigromante anywhere."

Will started at the name, then glanced at Kate; but she did not appear to have caught the connection.

"Go along home," Will murmured. The man went.

Will headed away from the George in the direction of London Bridge. Kate hurried after.

"Will, you'll never find one person on the streets of London at this time of night." She gave a short impatient huff. "You wouldn't be able to find him in the daytime."

That's for certain, Will thought.

Kate ran to keep up, then ran faster until she appeared in front of him and stopped, putting a hand to his chest so that he would stop too. "Do you think Nigromante is the one we're searching for?"

"I know he is," Will said.

"*How* do you know?"

"Because Nigromante means necromancer."

"Hell," Kate muttered.

"Exactly," Will agreed, and continued walking.

He could find the fiend in the dark. He had an affinity for the dead. Sooner or later, either Will or Guy de Nigromante would be drawn to the other, then—

Will saw a figure on the bridge and knew it was he.

"Stay here," he ordered, then raced away before Kate could protest.

He felt a slight twinge at leaving her behind, but she would be safer, even facing a dozen zombies, than joining him to face Nigromante.

"Will!" Kate shouted, but her voice was already fading as he turned the corner, then increased his speed in pursuit of the long, slim shadow in the distance. "You get back here!"

He half expected her to stomp her foot. Perhaps she did. The sudden ringing of a church bell drowned out her next words.

Following the sound, Will found his quarry on top of Southwark Cathedral. Will stared up; Nigromante stared down. He wore a long, black cape that made him appear bat-like and sinister. How pretentious! The myth that vampires could become bats was just that.

"Join me, Will!" He swept his cape aside theatrically. Was the man auditioning?

Will cursed. How was it that Nigromante seemed to know him, yet Will had just discovered *his* existence in the past hour?

Will used the stairs, even though Nigromante's mocking words followed him the whole way. "Will, Will, use your skill!"

Certainly he could climb the church wall, but what would he say to anyone who might see? *Yes, I, Will Shakespeare, have amazing vampire powers!*

Will thought not.

By the time he had reached the highest point of the cathedral, Nigromante sat on the edge. Will quashed the sudden urge to run forward and toss the necro-vampire to the street below. The fall wouldn't kill him. But Will knew what would.

His weapon cleared the scabbard in the blink of an eye. However, Nigromante moved even faster, and Will's blade sliced the tail end of the cape.

Will whirled, sword at the ready, but Nigromante stood out of reach, contemplating Will with an amused smile. "You need blood, Shakespeare. You're weak, and you're slow."

Nigromante appeared exactly as the man from the George had described him; however, his accent was English, not Spanish. Still, a Spaniard hung on his family tree somewhere. His appearance and his name shouted it; his treacherous behavior ensured it.

"You're new and stupid," Will said. "They're talking all over town about the wild animal that's been ripping out throats." Will shook his head. "And that cape." He moved a little closer. "Drawing attention to yourself is a good way to die young."

"Who would kill me?" Nigromante smirked. "You?"

"I will try."

"You will fail."

"You've already been captured once." Will's lip curled. "And by humans."

Nigromante tilted one inky black brow. "I was not a vampire then."

Will had wondered how Nigromante could have been imprisoned when he was so much stronger, faster, and more vicious than anyone alive, and why he'd allowed himself to be "killed" at all.

"You were changed within the walls of prison?" Will asked.

Nigromante's thin lips curved. "By whom?"

"Revealing that would be a fast way to a slow death."

Will could count on his fingers the number of undead he'd come across in his un-life. Vampires rarely made others like them. Most wanted to be the strongest and scariest of beings. Competition angered them, and when angered, they struck back. If two vampires fought, only one was left standing, which narrowed the ranks considerably.

If Nigromante was afraid of his maker, that vampire must be very old. Perhaps older than Will.

Will had no idea who that could be.

"Why die when you didn't have to?" Will asked.

"Part of the plan."

"You died, then came back to life," Will murmured, thinking aloud. "Once the plot against the Queen died with you, they wouldn't be looking for another so soon."

Nigromante shrugged, but Will knew he'd guessed right.

"I've been told of you," Nigromante said. "How you pretend to be human. How you take as little blood as you can, as if it is a strength to abstain and not a weakness."

"It *is* a strength," Will said quietly.

"How can that be when blood makes us superior to every being upon this earth?"

"It doesn't make us superior; it makes us base. The more human blood we take, the less human we become."

"If I'd wanted to stay human, I wouldn't have become a vampire." Nigromante sneered. "What's your excuse?"

Will didn't plan to share his reasons for becoming a vampire with this *enfant*. What he really wanted to do was kill him, but first he needed to find out Nigromante's plan for the Queen so that he could stop it.

"Do you not miss it?" Nigromante murmured. "The heat,

the taste, that flow of power through your veins? With enough blood, we can do anything."

"I doubt that," Will said.

Nigromante merely smiled and continued to speak with the voice of the serpent in the garden. "And when you take the blood of a woman while you're taking her, the whole world lights up."

"Not for her," Will muttered.

"Then you aren't doing it right."

Will didn't bother to answer. Nigromante was trying to infuriate him, and it was working. Will didn't like to remember how he'd behaved when he'd first been changed.

Very much like Nigromante.

"How did you learn about me?" the man murmured.

"I feel dead people," Will said. "Don't you?"

"Sometimes."

Will's brain tingled. *I see dead people.*

The voice of a child. Where had that come from?

The usual place, Will's overactive imagination. But what if there were a child who saw dead people, as Will had? Poor lad. Everyone would think him crazy. He would need a doctor, and what if the doctor were—

"Shakespeare!"

Will blinked. He'd gone away in his head again. He really had to stop that, or at least limit it to times when he wasn't facing a necro-vampire who could kill him.

"Perhaps if you ceased listening to the bloodlust," Will murmured, "and instead listened to the rhythm of the earth and its inhabitants, you'd hear more than your own selfish needs."

Nigromante snarled, flashing fangs. Will rolled his eyes.

Such behavior was wasted on him. He'd seen so many more frightening things in his lifetimes than a few sharp teeth.

"I don't want to," Nigromante said. "This city isn't big enough for both of us."

"If that's true, then why haven't you tried to kill me?"

"What do you think my zombies have been doing?"

"A very bad job," Will said. "I'm still alive."

More or less.

"You've had help." Nigromante pouted. He really was an annoying youngster. "How was I supposed to know there was a hunter in London?"

"Why wouldn't there be?"

"There are very few hunters left."

True. Will had yet to meet one as proficient as Kate—and most didn't have a vampire to help them when things got out of hand.

"I know you tried to kill the Queen," Will said.

"So?"

Will inched ever closer. The necro-vampire didn't seem to notice. "You'll try again."

Nigromante shrugged. "If they pay me."

"Who?"

Guy's lips curved. At least his fangs were no longer visible. "You think I'd tell you who hired me so that you could steal my job?"

"I would never hurt the Queen."

Guy's forehead creased. "Why not?"

"She's . . . the Queen." A few more steps, and Will was within hacking distance of Nigromante. Now if he could just keep him distracted.

"Not our Queen."

"My Queen," Will stated. "For as long as she lives."

Nigromante snorted. "Your humanity will be the death of you, Shakespeare."

"I do not agree. My humanity is what has kept me alive."

"Let's see," Nigromante said.

With one hand, Guy snatched Will off his feet, then he tossed him from the roof.

Chapter Thirty-five

"How bitter a thing it is to look into happiness through another man's eyes!"

—*As You Like It* (Act V, scene 2)

I tried to follow, but Will was too quick for me. I'd never seen him, or anyone else for that matter, run so fast.

Before he'd disappeared, he'd stared in the direction of London Bridge, so I headed that way. I found him unconscious on the street in front of Southwark Cathedral.

The night was so dark, and he was so still. At the first sight of him, I froze. If he was dead, what would I do?

Then he moved, and he moaned, and I was released from the inertia that had overcome me. I ran forward, then fell to my knees at his side.

"What happened?" Clouds covered the moon; I could barely see. But I knew well the scent of blood.

"I—" Will lifted a hand to his head, and his palm came away slick. "Not sure."

He slumped, and I gathered him against my chest like a child. "Did Nigromante hit you?"

My voice was rough; I heard the violence beneath the

words. If Guy de Nigromante were in front of me now, he would be the one bleeding.

"Nigromante," Will repeated, his breath warm upon my neck.

"The necro-vampire," I whispered. Not that there was anyone about, but one couldn't be too careful.

"Necro," he said, lips at my throat.

I shuddered as desire rose. What was he doing to me?

My head fell back as he drew my skin into his mouth and worried it, first with his tongue, then with his teeth.

Now I was the one who moaned. Right before Will tensed, then straightened with a startled, "Oh!" I could have sworn that he bit me just a little.

Will glanced up, then grabbed his head and swayed.

"Do not move so fast!" All I needed was for him to faint. He wasn't a large man, but I doubted I could drag him home. "Can you rise?"

Will seemed to realize of a sudden that he was sprawled in the middle of the road. "Of course," he said, and did. I kept a hand on his elbow just in case.

"Come along. I'll take you home."

"There's no place like home," Will muttered.

"What?"

"Nothing. Ah, no. Musn't go. Must *stay*. He's here somewhere. Can't you—" Will stumbled, and I grabbed his arm, drawing it around my shoulders.

"Can't I what?" I asked.

"Never mind," he muttered, and after a final glance about, he came along with me.

"You must have a care," he said. "Nigromante is dangerous.

If he guessed you were the one killing his zombies, he would most likely—"

"Kill me?" I interrupted. "I'd like to see him try." After what the bastard had done to Will, I couldn't wait to slice off his head.

"You have no idea what this fiend can do. Do not go looking for him without me." Will stopped, and I looked into his eyes. "Promise me, Kate."

"Of course," I said.

He reached out an unsteady hand and ran a night-cool finger beneath my eye. "The bruise," he murmured. "'Tis almost gone."

I'd forgotten about the black eye Nurse had given me. That he brought it up now only served to show his mind was muddled. He definitely needed to lie down.

We moved on, him giving me directions to his place, but the promise made me nervous. I glanced back, stuttering a step before I yanked my gaze to the front.

Had that been a figure atop the cathedral? Tall, thin, dark, with a cape that made him appear like a great black bat?

I shook my head, squeezed my eyes shut, then opened them.

The figure was gone. I was seeing things.

Or, as we were talking about a vampire, maybe not.

I wanted to question Will more, but he was so weak he could barely walk. I managed to save my interrogation until we reached his room, and I got him into bed.

He was nearly as pale as the sheets, his beard and eyes stark against them, the trail of blood from the wound on his forehead bright and fearsome.

I found a cloth and wet it with tepid water from his basin. As I washed his face, the questions came.

"What happened?" I asked again.

"I'm not sure." Will flinched as I hit a particularly sensitive spot, and when he opened his eyes, they were cast down. "I was chasing him, and the next thing I knew you were there, and I lay in the street."

"Head wounds will do that," I said. I'd had enough of them to know. Just because I was a very good chasseur didn't mean I hadn't received a bump and a bruise on more than one occasion.

"He must have hit you," I said. "Plank, stone. Something." I frowned at the wound, which continued to bleed. "I might need to stitch this, Will."

"No." He laid his head on the pillow and reached for the stained cloth. "'Twill stop soon enough."

I wasn't so sure about that, but I wasn't going to argue with him now.

"How did he get away?" I continued. "I wasn't that far behind."

Will shrugged, then winced at the movement.

"Where else does it hurt?"

"Where doesn't it hurt would be a better question," he muttered.

I reached for the laces on his doublet, and he brushed my hands away. "Leave it, Kate. I'll be fine in the morn."

I wanted to push, but I didn't. Time enough tomorrow to drag him by the ear to a physician if I felt that I needed to.

"I thought I saw—" I began.

Will's gaze flicked to my face. "What?"

Now I wasn't sure what I'd seen or if it even mattered.

A man on the parapet wearing a flowing black cape didn't mean that man had been Guy de Nigromante.

"Nothing," I said.

That Will let the matter drop proved to me more than the blood on his face that he was hurt deeper than he let on.

"What can I do for you, Will?" I put my hand on his arm. He pulled it away.

I glanced into his face just as his gaze lifted. Had he been staring at my breasts? Surely, he couldn't want me to do *that* when he was so weak.

Then again, I always felt so much better afterward. I lifted my hands and began to unfasten my own doublet.

"What are you doing?" Will's voice was choked.

"Crawling in beside you. You're chilled."

"Forsooth," he said. "I'm overly warm. Would you open the window?"

I did, then let the autumn breeze cool and calm me before I turned.

Will had fallen asleep.

Chapter Thirty-six

"We will draw the curtain and show you the picture."
—*Twelfth Night* (Act I, scene 5)

Will tried to slow his feigned breathing, to still his face and body, to appear asleep. He needed Kate to leave before he lost any semblance of control.

He was so weak. She was so strong. And so damn near.

Will stifled a sigh of desire. It had been nigh on a year since he'd fed. He wasn't sure he could resist her. Especially if she continued to hover over him, her lovely, smooth neck too close, that vein pulsing with life-giving scarlet—

Ay, marry! He would *not* drink from Kate. For if he did, she would know the truth, and that he could not bear.

Will knew he must have done an adequate job of pretending sleep, for Kate leaned over, kissed his brow, and left. *Praise the saints!*

He had a moment's unease at the thought of her out there with Guy de Nigromante on the loose, but she had been warned. Will could follow her, watch over her, protect her. But in truth, Will was more of a danger to Kate tonight than anyone or anything else upon this earth.

He was weak, and he was wounded. For a vampire, blood and lust, hunger and desire were all wrapped together, at times nearly impossible to distinguish from one another. If Will was vulnerable, as he was now, he would soon be unable to withstand the lure of any of them.

His body called out for nourishment. Soon the call would become a shout and the resistance painful. The only way he could heal quickly was if he took blood.

However, if he did, it would be quite obvious to Kate that he was mending abnormally fast. So he would abstain, and he would recover close to the incredibly slow rate of a human being.

Sweat broke out on Will's cool, cool skin. His fangs sprang free despite his resolve that they would not. He fought the nearly overwhelming urge to leave his room and seek a willing donor. There had never been a shortage of people happy to give away their blood for money. And if that failed, he could always "push."

But Will felt ashamed after partaking of nourishment in such a manner. He was stronger in mind and body. He was taking advantage. Considering the lust and desire that rode hand in hand with the craving and the act of assuaging it, he would feel even worse if he succumbed tonight. Taking blood from another would be a betrayal of Kate and everything that they meant to each other.

She was his love. He would share that intimate act with no one but her. And since he could *not* share it with her, he would not share at all.

Will rested until the first rays of daylight threatened the horizon, then he tumbled from the bed and across the room to his hidey-hole.

He had spent centuries putting his hunger to rest, but that morn only his deathlike sleep stopped that hunger from raging out of control.

Come the night, Will arose, bruised, his head still bleeding now and again. He hated healing like a human.

He wrote, but badly. He snarled his way through rehearsal. But he caught Kate whispering and pointing at his head and knew she was smoothing his way.

Like a wife.

God, he wished she could be his wife.

The thought only made Will snarl all the more.

Days passed, and Will healed. He finished the play and began full rehearsals. Each night, he and Kate would hunt. They had no luck discovering Nigromante. It was as if the fiend had dropped from the face of the earth.

His zombies were another story. Will and Kate killed enough of those to fill the Thames with ashes.

But as the days and nights became weeks, and the play was nearly ready to open, they spent more and more time searching and less and less time finding zombies.

With fewer and fewer seemingly sick unto dying, gibbering, walking corpses, the fear of the plague faded. Even though more and more people were out and about, fewer and fewer disappeared. Rumor even had it that the Queen would soon return to London.

"I know he is somewhere in the city," Will insisted.

"You keep saying that," Kate said. "But *how* do you know?"

Rehearsals for *Two Gentlemen of Verona* were complete, and

it was time for the opening. The play would be a success, or it would be a failure, but open it would.

In an hour.

Will was a little nervous.

He'd been distracted while writing the manuscript—by Kate, by Nigromante, by the zombies, by Valentine and Proteus themselves. The two of them had dropped in and out, arguing half the night about what had happened and what had not. In the end, Will just made things up.

As a result, he wasn't certain about this play. Either it was the best thing he'd ever done, or the worst. He had no idea.

Which merely meant it was like every other play he'd ever written. He'd done what he could with what he had at the time, and whether the work was a success or a failure was no longer in his hands.

Or at least it wouldn't be in an hour.

He and Kate were getting dressed—Will as Valentine in a doublet of dark green wool with breeches a shade lighter. He'd chosen the color, as he'd thought an outlaw, which Valentine eventually became, would need to blend into the forest where he hid.

On the other hand, Kate as Silvia, the daughter of a duke, was dressed near to royalty. She'd brought her own clothes from home. They never would have been able to afford such at the Rose.

Kate wore jewels of gold, which brought out the honey hue of her skin, at last healed of every bruise. Her gown deep russet, the bodice cut to reveal the fine line of her collarbone, the waist small in contrast to the bell shape of her skirt, the color a perfect complement to the ebony gleam of her hair. In it, she was the most beautiful woman he had ever seen.

Too bad he couldn't trust her with his truth.

So Will sighed, and he lied some more. "I know because Nigromante would not disappear from London when he has a job to do."

"He failed in his assignment. He was caught and executed for treason."

"But he isn't *dead*, Kate."

She patted her hair, which she'd swept into some fancy twist no one in his company would ever have been able to accomplish. "His zombies are."

Will couldn't argue that they'd done an excellent job ridding the city of the risen dead. Nevertheless, Will remained uneasy. Though he hadn't seen any in days, he still felt the dead all around him. Had he become paranoid along with everything else?

Kate believed he was merely anxious about the play, which was true. Both that and the odd tingle at the back of his brain gave him a greasy, grimy feeling in his stomach. Perhaps once they got past the opening, the strange sensation would go away.

Or maybe he should just vomit and get it over with.

"Calm yourself, Will." Kate set her hand on his arm. "Everything will be fine."

He wanted to believe her, but he didn't.

"You seem tired," she said.

"Love hath chased sleep from my enthrallèd eyes," he muttered, "and made them watchers of mine own heart's sorrow."

"Love's a mighty lord," she returned, "and hath so humbled me, as, I confess, there is no woe to his correction, nor to his service no such joy on earth."

Will had to smile. "That isn't even your part," he said. 'Twas his. Did she know every word in the entire play? He wouldn't be surprised.

"Tell me." Her fingers stroked him through the cloth. "What is your favorite line?"

She was trying to distract him. Will was in such a state he let her.

"And why not death rather than living torment?"

Kate laughed, understanding that he referred to his nerves about the play, the zombies, the Queen, everything.

"To die is to be banish'd from myself," he continued, "and Silvia is myself; banish'd from her is self from self: a deadly banishment!"

She nodded encouragingly, her lips parted just so, kissable if he was of a mind to kiss. He was, though not quite yet.

"What light is light, if Silvia be not seen? What joy is joy, if Silvia be not by? Unless it be to think that she is by and feed upon the shadow of perfection."

He touched her cheek, and she sighed, eyes drifting closed, mouth lifting in expectation.

"Except I be by Silvia in the night," he whispered, "there is no music in the nightingale; unless I look on Silvia in the day, there is no day for me to look upon; she is my essence."

Their lips met at last, and Will sank into the sweet, sweet taste of love. What he would give for this, for her, for always.

Everything. Anything.

Kate lifted her mouth from his, and murmured, "O Valentine, *this* I endure for thee!"

Will laughed, and for the first time in weeks he felt at peace. Perhaps Kate was right, and everything *would* be fine.

He lowered his head, determined to kiss Kate until

someone made him stop, and there came a knock on the door. "Master Shakespeare. On the stage, please!"

Damn. He'd thought he would have more time.

Though the first scene was Will's and Ned's, as Valentine and Proteus, respectively, nevertheless Kate took Will's hand and walked with him to the wings.

Ned already stood behind the curtain. He scowled in Will's direction when he saw him with Kate. Ned did not care to have romances between the cast. But Will no longer cared what Ned liked, or anyone else for that matter. Life, or in his case, death, was too short.

He kissed Kate's mouth, tweaked her nose, and joined Ned on the stage.

"Shakespeare," Ned growled, "you push me too far."

Will began to make some retort, he knew not what, and stilled. Death lounged nearby. He could barely breathe from the smell.

The curtain lifted.

Nothing but zombies stared back at him.

Chapter Thirty-seven

"The worst is not, so long as we can say,
'This is the worst.'"

—*King Lear* (Act IV, scene I)

I could tell from the way Will froze, then glanced my way, eyes wide, face pale, that something was wrong.

I began to go to him, even though I would be fired within seconds of stepping onto the stage ahead of my cue, but a loud call came from the balcony.

"All hail, the Queen."

"Bugger me," Will muttered loud enough to be heard backstage.

"Shakespeare!" Ned snapped. "Are ye daft, man? The Queen."

"Kate!" Will shouted.

"Not Kate," Ned whispered furiously. "He's Silvia. And it's not his turn. 'Tis you and me now, *Valentine.*"

Ned thought Will had forgotten his lines. From my point of view, Will appeared to have forgotten his name. Whatever he'd seen in the audience had turned him ghost white. I had a pretty good idea what it was.

I snatched up my sword and one for Will too. Just because I'd believed we were almost free of zombies didn't mean I went anywhere unprepared. I kept weapons nearby and wore breeches under my costume.

"Cease to persuade, my loving Proteus," Ned encouraged, loudly and slowly.

I sliced my fine wool dress, along with the shift beneath, from ankle to belly, then ripped them off at the waist. Once they were gone, the padded roll at my hips, which kept the skirt in a bell shape, fell to the floor. Thus freed, I stepped onto the stage.

We were surrounded on three sides. Not a single living being occupied the ground-floor space; above, only the Queen and her attendants leaned forward eagerly.

As always, the Queen dazzled, in a forest green gown embroidered with gold. A gold ruff encircled her neck, and jewels sparkled on her hands, at her throat, ears, even in her hair. Though the dark color of her clothing showed she was dressed for an outing, nevertheless the wide skirt, floor-length cape, and elaborate coif would never allow her to run.

As if I would ask a nearly sixty-year-old woman to run, even if she weren't the Queen of England.

I tossed Will a rapier. He caught it in one hand, and together we faced the horde.

I'd never seen so many zombies in one place. There had to be nigh onto a hundred. Where had Nigromante been hiding them?

"What is the matter with you?" Ned began to wrestle with Will for possession of the weapon. "No swordplay yet."

"Ned," Will said between gritted teeth, gaze on the advancing zombies, "not now. Run away."

"Proteus runs from no one!" Ned announced, drawing himself up to his impressive height and allowing his lovely voice to flow free. He slapped Will on the back of the head and repeated, more loudly and more slowly than before, "Cease to persuade, my loving Proteus!"

Will smacked the hilt of his sword into Ned's temple. Alleyn went down like a felled horse.

Will's eyes met mine, and he shrugged. Then his attention was drawn to the zombies, which had begun to chant: "Br-br-br—!"

The gaze of each and every one was fixed on an unconscious Ned Alleyn.

"Bad idea," I said, and grabbed the man's leg. "Get the other one!" I ordered as the first tibonage scrambled over the edge of the stage.

"Why are they after him? They crave *fresh* brains."

"He isn't dead, Will. Just insensible. To them he's supper."

"Right." Will sighed and picked up Ned's other leg. "Bad idea."

We dragged Ned—which wasn't easy; he was huge—to the wings and handed him to the horrified cast and crew.

"What has happened?" Edmond asked.

I opened my mouth, then shut it again. I had no idea what to say. Will had no such problem.

"Attack of the plague monsters," he said. "Run!"

They ran.

"Wait," Will called. "Take Ned!"

But they were already gone.

Will cursed and glanced back. Half a dozen zombies had made their way onto the stage.

"Hide him," Will said, and waded in.

I dumped Ned off the edge and, grunting and sweating, managed to roll him beneath. Then I leaped into the fray.

I'd be lying if I said I didn't enjoy myself. This was what I'd been born to do, and I was good at it. Together, Will and I were damn near invincible.

"Ha!" I shouted, and sliced through the neck of what appeared to be a yeoman farmer. He didn't even have time to look surprised before he burst into ashes.

The sound of clapping drew my attention upward. The Queen's ladies cooed and tittered and whispered excitedly to one another. What was wrong with them? They should be running for their lives.

Will killed another tibonage, and when the ashes rained down, the ladies applauded again like this was part of the—

"Play," I muttered, then used my sword to backhand a zombie that either thought I was blind on my right side or just stupid. I'd seen him creeping up on me for the past few minutes.

"Will," I said, a bit breathless. I'd been working hard.

"Kate," he returned, not breathless at all, and he'd killed more of the tibonage than I had since I'd lost time hiding Ned Alleyn. How did he do that?

"They think this is part of the play."

"Who does?" Will asked.

"The Queen." I lifted my chin to indicate the balcony, even as I twirled and kicked out with one leg, knocking a zombie through the paper wall that hung at the back of the stage. Then I sliced the head off the one that had stood right next to him.

The Queen wasn't clapping or laughing. She wasn't giggling or twittering. I doubted she ever had. No, the Queen was watching Will and me kill zombies as if her life depended on it.

She had always been a very smart queen.

"Shouldn't we get her out of here?" I shouted.

Will didn't answer. Instead, he began to fight his way toward Her Majesty, and suddenly I understood.

We'd made a very large dent in the crowd of the dead. If we cut a swath through the center, we could then race up the stairs and protect the Queen. The zombies would follow, but the narrowness of the staircase would inhibit their movement, and we could pick them off two by two until they were gone, keeping the Queen and her ladies behind us and safe all the while.

Which is exactly what Will and I did. Or tried to.

We had just reached the stairs when a commotion near the open area of the theater arose, and more zombies swarmed in.

Will and I took one look at each other and ran upward, but as we gained the top level we came face-to-face with Guy de Nigromante.

Chapter Thirty-eight

"To be, or not to be: That is the question."
—*Hamlet* (Act III, scene I)

Will wanted to grab Kate and shove her behind him, except there were zombies crowding the stairwell. If he put her in front of him, she'd be closer to Nigromante. What to do, what to do?

Will solved the dilemma by dragging her alongside him when he put himself between the Queen and the vampire assassin.

Nigromante was covered in blood. His fangs were out, pressing against his too-red lips like the tips of twin knives against a strawberry. The Queen's guards lay in pieces. They'd never stood a chance.

"I'm stronger than you, Shakespeare." Nigromante closed in. "You'll never win."

His face flushed with fresh blood, his muscles bulged against the material of his black doublet, and his shoulders strained the seams. The blood he'd imbibed, both recently and in the past, gave him strength, speed, agility. Will might be older, but Nigromante was right.

He couldn't win. Not like this.

"You could be strong too." Nigromante's lovely, lilting, tempting voice slid around Will like a snake. His gaze flicked beside Will to Kate, and he smirked. "All you'd have to do is—"

"Shut up," Will said, low and furious.

But Nigromante didn't have to listen to him. One such as he listened to no one.

"Drink from her, Shakespeare. You know that you want to."

Will felt Kate stiffen. "What is he talking about, Will?"

"She doesn't know?" Nigromante asked, then he began to laugh. "Ah, Shakespeare, you *are* a fool."

Will didn't dare take his eyes from the necro-vampire. He was going to die, no doubt, but Will did not plan to give up. He'd fight to save Kate and his Queen.

"Stall," the Queen murmured. "Help will come."

Unfortunately, help would probably end up in pieces on the floor the same as the last help had. Regardless, stalling sounded like a good idea to Will, and the Queen *had* commanded it. Who knew what might happen if he had a little more time.

"If you're so damnably strong," Will asked, "why didn't you kill me before now?"

"You don't know?" Nigromante tilted his head with a strange, almost birdlike motion. "I suppose not, or you wouldn't have walked right into this."

"Into what?" Kate asked, drawing the vampire's gaze. His eyes widened, and he licked his lips. The ruined costume was quite fetching. Her breeches clung to her limbs below the waist, and what was left of her dress revealed too much of her chest above.

Will wanted to shout for Kate to be silent. The more attention she drew to herself, the more interested in her Nigromante would become. Death at Will's side would be less of a horror than Nigromante's hunger.

"I raised a small group of zombies," Nigromante answered, gaze still caught upon the curve of Kate's neck revealed by her ripe, russet gown, "then I sent them after Master Shakespeare."

They'd been correct in that deduction. What they'd never understood was why.

"I knew he'd kill them." Nigromante lifted his lip in a horrible parody of a smile and revealed the sharp length of his fangs.

Out of the corner of his eye, Will saw the Queen shudder. Her fate was sealed unless—

But no! There had to be another way. Will could not, would not—

"Why would you do that?" Kate asked.

"Kate," Will murmured. "Shh."

Nigromante's expression became arch. He knew why Will wanted Kate's silence, and it amused him.

"Every time I raise a few zombies," he continued, "rumors of the plague begin, and the Queen flees." Nigromante cast Elizabeth an annoyed glance. "I decided to use that fear."

"Let everyone believe the plague has come," Will said, "then when I kill off enough zombies, they'll think it has passed, and the Queen will return."

"Why didn't you just raise, then kill them yourself?" Kate asked.

Did the woman never *listen*?

"I had hopes they would end *him*"—Nigromante lifted his chin in Will's direction—"and spare me the trouble. But you were always around to save him."

"It's what I do," she said.

"Not for long."

Kate snorted, and the fiend's eyes flared.

"You could not have known," Elizabeth interrupted, "that I would come to the Rose today."

"But obviously I did know." Nigromante swept a deep, yet sarcastic bow. "Those around you are not as loyal as you would believe."

Will glanced at the Queen as she paled. Poor woman. She was forever the victim of plots and schemes and subterfuge. Whom could she trust? Robert Dudley, her dearest friend, was dead. She had little family left, and most of those would take the throne from her if given any chance at all.

Elizabeth was old, though no one would dare tell her that. Not if they valued their heads. She was both her mother's and her father's daughter in appearance as well as in cunning and strength.

Anne Boleyn's snapping dark eyes peered out of a now-lined-yet-regal face. The Queen's hands were Anne's too—though devoid of the sixth finger that was her mother's curse. Long and slim, unbelievably graceful, they drew attention whenever she moved them.

The flaming red hair of Henry VIII rose above Elizabeth's high forehead, adorned in pearls, a sparkling jeweled cap pinned to the top. Some said the Queen's hair was thin, almost gone, that the coif she presented to the world was a wig. If so, it was a very good one, as Will could not tell the difference between her hair now and when she had been newly crowned.

"The latest play by Shakespeare is not something you would neglect forever," Nigromante continued. "Had you not come today, there was always tomorrow, and tomorrow, and tomorrow."

Damnation! Trapped by her love of his work.

"Where did you keep the army hidden?"

Kate again. Will smacked himself in the head with the flat of his hand. Everyone ignored him.

"A ship," Nigromante answered, "up the Thames, just off the coast."

"You could afford a ship large enough to hide several hundred un-men?" Will asked.

"No." Nigromante lifted a brow as he waited for Will to make the connection.

"King Philip could."

The Queen made a small, startled sound, and Nigromante's smile bloomed. "When the King decides on something, he sees it through." Nigromante dipped his head. "As do I."

Though it had never been proven that Nigromante had been paid by King Philip of Spain to kill the Queen, everyone in England had known it was true. The necro-vampire had just confirmed it.

"He never did get over the Armada," Will muttered.

"Would you?" Nigromante asked.

Will didn't answer. His gaze remained on the increasing horde of zombies. He had to find a way to get Kate and the Queen, as well as her ladies, out of here alive. Right now the prospects were slim.

"Enough talk." Nigromante reached for one of Elizabeth's ladies, who cringed, shrieked, and ran.

Nigromante became a blur, and when he materialized again, he stood in front of the woman. She looked into his eyes, and she was lost. "Go to them." He pointed at the zombies.

"No!" Will shouted, but it was too late. Without even a blink of her eye in protest, the woman walked into the eager embrace of the zombie horde.

Her screams, the sounds of teeth slashing, flesh tearing were sickening. Even more so when punctuated by Nigromante's half-mad laughter.

"You." The fiend pointed at a second lady. "Jump." He pointed to the balcony's edge. Will threw himself forward, but he wasn't close enough to catch her before she fell into the waiting crowd below. The air became heavy with the scent of blood and the sounds of a feast.

"One, two, three," Nigromante announced, then pointed the remaining ladies toward the rest of the ravenous herd.

"What are they doing?" Kate cried.

"He has power over human minds."

Kate cursed and brought up her rapier. Will caught her as she ran past.

"No, Kate," he said as she fought him. He held her, legs off the ground, arms pinned to her sides.

"He's killing them."

"He'll do the same to you."

She stilled. "I think he's going to anyway, Will."

She was right. Unless he increased his strength, they would all die here.

Will suddenly found himself leaning forward, lips a

hairsbreadth from the pulsing vein in Kate's neck, teeth itching as they lengthened.

He jerked away. Counted to five, thought of . . . puppies. He had no taste for them. In seconds, his teeth stopped growing.

There *was* another way. There just had to be.

"Do not be so foolish."

Will stiffened as the melodic voice seemed to rise above the chaos in the room. Nounou stood behind Nigromante.

"I would help you if I could." She swung a fist at the fiend's head. Her hand passed right through.

Nigromante stiffened, frowned, glanced upward, then downward, then left and right. He shook his head and yanked on one ear.

"You will have to help yourself dis time. Do whatever you have to do."

"She'll hate me," Will said.

"Will?" Kate stilled in his arms. "Who are you talking to?"

Nigromante turned and nearly jumped out of his boots at the sight of the tall, regal black woman standing directly behind him. He swiped at her with his sword, then smirked when his blade had no effect.

"I'd listen to her, Shakespeare."

"Listen to who?" Kate fairly shouted.

The necro-vampire looked Nounou up and down. "Tall, Moorish woman. Brightly colored . . ." He moved his hand, indicating flowing robes and something on the head.

"Nounou," Kate murmured, and in her voice Will heard her pain.

"There's a lot he didn't tell you, sweet Kate."

Hearing his own name for her on that man's lips made Will's vision waver in fury. He should have told her, tried to explain—though what explanation there was for one such as he, Will had no idea—but when his vision misted with red, he could do nothing but kill.

Will stared into Kate's eyes and did what he'd sworn he would not. "Stay," he ordered.

When he stepped back, she resembled the women who had so recently met their deaths at the hands of zombies.

"Never say her name," he muttered. "Never."

Nigromante just laughed. Will tightened his grip on the rapier.

"What do you plan to do?" the Queen asked.

"Kill him."

"He says you cannot."

"He says a lot of things. I choose not to listen."

The Queen's lips curved. "I've always liked you, Master Shakespeare. I'd hate to see you walking about without a head."

"You won't," he promised. Because without a head, he could not walk.

"If you succeed in killing the assassin, what about those—" Her lip curled. Her gaze touched on the zombies, then skittered away. "Things."

"Perhaps they will disappear once he's dead."

"Do you really think that could happen?"

Will's gaze met the Queen's. "A vampire raised zombies in a plot to kill the Queen of England, madam. In my opinion, anything could happen."

"You're right," she said. "Carry on."

Will turned away, but at her quiet "Will?" he turned back.

"Do not die." She gave him a small, sad smile. "I command it."

He didn't have the heart to tell her he was already dead.

"Your Majesty," he said, and bowed.

Seconds later, Will and Guy clashed swords. They strained, each trying to shove the other backward so he could thrust or slice.

"I should kill you," Guy muttered. "But I want you to watch. I want you to see them both die by my hand."

"You aren't going to order them to sacrifice themselves to your zombie horde?" Will sneered, even though Guy was steadily pushing him backward. Will might be better with a sword; unfortunately, such skill mattered not when Guy was stronger and faster.

"Where would be the fun in that?" Guy's eyes flared. "I've heard royal blood is intoxicating. I can't wait to find out."

The thought of this fiend's mouth on the neck of his monarch sickened Will. The thought of that mouth on Kate made him roar with fury. Will attempted to throw Nigromante backward so he could chop off his head in a single swipe. Instead, Nigromante threw Will across the room with one jerk of his shoulder, and Will realized—

Guy had merely been playing with him.

Will hit the floor hard enough to knock the wind out of him, if he'd had any wind *in* him. Nevertheless, he was stunned. He didn't move quickly enough, and Nigromante landed on his chest.

Before Will could even try to defend himself, the vampire leaned over and used his teeth to tear a very large hole in Will's throat.

Blood sprayed. The fiend stuck his mouth beneath the

flow as if it were a champagne fountain. Will felt his life, such that it was, ebbing away.

If he'd been strong enough, he could have healed the wound in an instant. If he had human blood now, he might yet survive.

But he *could* not drink from the Queen, and he *would* not drink from his love.

Darkness hovered all around, looming larger, coming closer, as Will whispered one last time, "Kate."

And the spell upon her was broken.

Chapter Thirty-nine

"Off with his head!"
—*Richard III* (Act III, scene 4)

Kate.

Will whispered my name, and I woke up, shook my head, blinked. Had I really been asleep?

"God's periwig," I muttered. Blood and zombies were everywhere. How could I have lost time right in the middle of a battle?

One of the tibonage tossed what appeared to be a bloody ball to another. However, when the second started sucking on it, I realized he held a head that had previously belonged to one of the Queen's ladies.

"Will?" I murmured.

"He's weakening."

I turned to Elizabeth. She was pale, which was saying a lot considering she'd been ghostly to begin with. The rouge on her cheeks and lips stood out as starkly as the blood all over the floor. Her orange hair blazed brighter even than the carnage. Pupils huge with shock, the Queen's eyes appeared as dark as a moonless summer night.

"Help him," she said.

I followed her gaze. Will lay on the floor. Or at least I thought it was Will. I could barely see him for the blood. There appeared to be more outside than in, and what was left Nigromante was drinking.

What had happened before time had paused for me? Will had said, "Stay," and the next thing I knew, I'd heard my name and awoken.

My fingers curled into fists, even as another memory came. Will speaking to Nounou, who'd been dead for months.

I added those two clues together and came up with—

"Necro-vampire." No wonder Will had known so much about them.

"He needs blood," Elizabeth murmured.

She seemed quite calm considering there were zombies milling about, and two vampires lay in a puddle of blood on the floor. I was impressed. I wanted to—

"Kill somebody." I bent and picked up my sword.

"Not Will," the Queen ordered. "Save him." She drew herself up, the jewels on her gown sparkling in the misty late-afternoon light. "I command it, boy."

At least she still thought I was a young man in the guise of a woman. If we ever got out of this, I'd hate to find myself in jail for walking onto a stage.

"Yes, Your Majesty," I said, roughening my voice to give the masquerade more weight.

Since Nigromante was occupied sucking on Will's neck—how disgusting—I walked up behind him and proceeded to slice through his neck.

Unfortunately, he heard me coming and threw himself to the side. I didn't get a clean slice. His head hung by a thread.

I might be a brave, tough chasseur, but that was too much for me. I yanked my gaze from Nigromante, then I found I couldn't look away from Will.

He was so still. So pale and yet so . . . red. My chest ached. I had loved him.

"Past tense," I muttered. He was not the man I'd believed him to be.

Hell, he wasn't even a man at all.

Though I didn't think blood loss would kill a vampire, it was obvious that I knew little about them. Right now, Will appeared already dead.

I inched closer, my shoes slipping in the mess on the floor. What should I do?

"He needs blood," the Queen repeated. "It will strengthen him, heal him."

How did she know so damn much about it?

The zombies hovered, awaiting Nigromante's command. The necro-vampire writhed on the floor, bleeding, but even as I watched, he began to heal.

I cursed, dipped my finger in a puddle, and held it to Will's lips.

The Queen made an impatient sound. "That is not good enough. He needs fresh, warm blood. Offer him yourself."

"I already have," I murmured. I'd offered him everything, and he'd taken it.

Not everything.

Was that Nounou's voice? Or did I just want it to be?

"Boy!" the Queen said urgently. "You must hurry!"

Nearly a dozen zombies surrounded Nigromante, their flat, dead gazes fixed on me. Once the fiend healed, he would either order my death or see to it himself.

In that moment, my broken heart hurt so badly, I would have welcomed death. However, I could not allow them to touch the Queen.

"The only one who can save us now, child, is—"

"Will," I said, and he opened his eyes.

Chapter Forty

"Cowards die many times before their deaths;
the valiant never taste of death but once."

—*Julius Caesar* (Act II, scene 2)

Kate stood above him, her head haloed by the setting sun. "Drink from me," she said.

Was he dead?

Reaching up, Will felt his throat. It hurt! It bled.

Definitely not dead, but from the lethargy in his limbs, the confusion in his head, he would be too weak to stop Nigromante from finishing him off whenever he wished to.

Which would most likely be right after he made Will watch him first torture, then kill Kate and the Queen.

Kate fell to her knees. She slid in the blood and skidded into Will's side, jostling his body so hard he moaned.

"Sorry," she muttered, though she didn't sound sorry at all. "The Queen commands that I save you."

She leaned closer, the neck of her dress pulled low, her breasts in his face.

"No," he managed.

She leaned back on her heels, her exasperation evident. "I

incapacitated Nigromante, but that won't last forever." Her lips tightened as if she didn't want to say the next words, but she did anyway. "Help us, Will Shakespeare; you're our only hope."

Will's head tilted as the words seemed to swirl all around him. What a great line for a play . . .

Dizzy as he was with blood loss, his mind wandered to a galaxy far, far away. Battles in flying machines. An old warrior. A young one who needed training. A girl. No. A *princess.* Perhaps a mystical force—

"Will! Now is not the time to drift away to the stories in your head."

How did she know that was what he had done? Because Kate knew him better than anyone. Though not well enough if she thought he would ever drink from her sweet veins.

She leaned close again, the long, thin blue line in her neck hovering directly above his lips. "Drink," she ordered.

"No."

"We will all die, Will." She pressed her skin to his mouth.

His fangs erupted, cutting his own lips, but no blood flowed. He'd already lost too much. Darkness flickered at the edge of his vision.

"No," he whispered.

She sat up. Her eyes met his. "You must," she said, then before he knew what she was about, she drew his dagger and slit her own throat.

To his horror, blood spurted everywhere, some landing on Will and causing him to break out in a cold sweat. Kate's eyelids fluttered, and she sank gracefully to the floor.

"Now you have no choice," a voice said.

"You're still here?" Will muttered.

"Where would I go?" Nounou asked.

Will almost said, *To hell,* but Nounou was powerful. She could probably send *him* there. And while Will didn't mind dying to keep Kate safe, he did mind dancing in the flames for all eternity yet not saving her at all.

"You must drink, or she will die."

The ghost was right. Kate was bleeding so badly she needed the healing properties of his saliva to heal, just as he needed her blood to gain enough strength to save them all.

Will cursed Nigromante, the Queen, the zombies, even Kate herself, but he knew what he must do.

Her taste was ripe grapes in the sun, red wine in golden goblets during the depths of a winter night. Power flowed into him, both energy and might. He kept drinking. She was so tasty, and it had been so very long.

"Stop, Will."

He couldn't. It was as he'd feared. Once he'd begun to drink from Kate, he could not cease. She was temptation. Desire. The darkness he fought every day.

"Will! Time now to stop." He shrugged Nounou's hand from his shoulder—not hard considering it wasn't really there—and sank his fangs ever deeper into Kate's flesh.

"You love her. Dat love is stronger dan your beast. *You* are stronger dan dat. T'ink of her."

Kate's face appeared in his mind, the sound of her laughter, the sweet scent of roses, her gentle touch. It was easy to remember her; she was now a part of him.

Will lifted his head. His gaze fell on her wound. Lowering his head, he swept his tongue along it, fighting the demon that told him to drink a little more; what could it hurt?

The wound closed within seconds. Now, if he waited until she opened her eyes, he could make her forget this had ever happened.

But he wouldn't. She had the right to hate him forever for what he'd done. He couldn't take that from her. If she was to love him, she must love him despite what he was. Will knew the chance of that was very slim, but he would take that chance. He'd rather have no love at all than a love that wasn't real.

Will was suddenly yanked violently upward and tossed across the room. He grappled for purchase, trying to stop himself before he smashed into something hard enough to stun. His arms twirled so quickly and with such force, he changed direction. Retracing his flight through the air, he crashed into Nigromante just as the fiend reached for Kate.

The two tumbled to the floor. Will grabbed the man by the throat and bashed his head against the planks to the rhythm of his words.

"Never." *Thunk.* "Touch." *Thunk.* "Her." *Thunk. Thunk. Thunk.* "Kill. Them. A—"

Will tore the necro-vampire's head from his shoulders and tossed it away.

Frightened that he might be tempted again, Will leaped back before the blood hit him in the face. He glanced around for the head and discovered it had rolled across the floor, stopping only inches from the Queen.

She stared at Nigromante's shocked face, then she took one step forward and kicked it with all her might. Despite the dainty foot and the satin slipper upon it, the head sailed up and over Will, falling with a wet plop in the center of the zombie horde.

They fell on it like starving wild animals.

The Queen rubbed her hands together. "I enjoyed that." Her gaze met Will's. "Finish them," she ordered. "Before they finish us."

Several hundred zombies were no match for a necro-vampire who'd just taken fresh blood. Will mowed his way through them with his rapier, his hands, and his teeth. By the time he made it down the stairs and into the group below, he was so covered with ash and dust that a cloud poofed around him with every step.

The zombies kept trying to drive past him and up the stairs to the women. He did not let one single fiend succeed.

At last, Will stood in the middle of a very dirty theater all alone. Or at least he was alone until Ned Alleyn popped up through the trapdoor. He took one look at Will and began to scream.

"Fie," Will muttered. "Puppies, puppies, puppies." His fangs retracted.

Will stepped forward; Alleyn stumbled back. Will caught the man's eyes. "Halt," he said. When the man did, though he did not stop screaming, Will murmured, "Quiet."

The screaming ceased.

"Go home and forget everything that you saw here."

Ned turned and walked away.

Will remained on his stage. The Rose appeared as if it had been used by a farmer to slaughter cattle. A farmer who had then burned everything still left to ashes. It would take weeks to set the place right.

At a loss, Will just stood there in the middle of the carnage. A movement, a sound, he knew not which, caused him to glance up.

His eyes met Kate's, and in that instant, he knew he had lost her.

Chapter Forty-one

"Now is the winter of our discontent."
—*Richard III* (Act I, scene I)

Until I saw Will with Ned, proving he could control minds, I'd been hoping I was wrong, that he hadn't been controlling me. But faced with the evidence, I had no choice but to believe, and once I believed, I began to question everything.

Was the love I'd felt for him real? Would I ever be able to trust my own heart again? I knew I couldn't trust him.

"Kate," he whispered.

I straightened and turned away.

The Queen's gaze was sharp upon me. "What is your name, boy?"

"Clayton, Your Majesty."

She moved closer, her eyes narrowing. Then, before I knew what she was about, she withdrew several pins from my hair. It tumbled all around me. The Queen grabbed a handful and yanked.

"Ouch!" I scowled. So did she.

"Your name is not Clayton, I'll trow."

"Kate!" Will came up the stairs. He ran across the distance between us.

I brought up my rapier. Not that it would harm him.

Unless I cut off his head.

"Kate?" the Queen murmured.

Will's eyes widened as he realized what he had done. I shrugged. Right now, I didn't care if I spent the rest of my life in jail. Preferable to spending it with Reginald.

"Katherine Dymond, Your Majesty." I began to bow, but quickly changed the movement to a curtsy.

"Dymond." The Queen's eyes narrowed. "Your father would be Charles Wintour."

I opened my mouth, shut it again. How did she know that?

"The Charles Wintour who recently bought a barony for his daughter and son-in-law?"

"I—" I glanced at Will, all blood and ashes and anguish, then quickly away. "I do not know of it, Your Majesty."

"You soon will, as I was told your husband"—she turned her gaze on Will—"should soon be home. Any day."

Will muttered a word that caused the Queen's thin eyebrows to lift.

Heavy footsteps sounded below. Had someone at last noticed the Queen missing and sent troops?

"Mistress! My lady! Child!"

Nurse's voice was, as usual, far too loud. All three of us winced at the volume.

"What is she doing out of her cage?" Will asked.

The Queen cast him a quick glance. Will ducked his head. "Not a real cage," he muttered.

Nurse ascended the steps onto the stage, peered up, and

saw me. "Ach, there ye are." Then her gaze went to Will. "Doctor Caius, what're ye doin' here?"

"Dere was a sickness," Will said in the voice of Caius. "But dey are all gone now."

"Gone?" Nurse echoed. She glanced around the disgusting stage and paled. "Dead?"

Will stuck his nose into the air. "Sometimes even a doctor such as I cannot save people from de plague. You, good nurse, are a miracle!"

The Queen snorted, then looked back and forth between Will and me. "I know not what you two have been doing"—she lifted a brow—"though I have a good idea."

"My lady, you must come home!" Nurse shouted. "The master has arrived."

My heart tumbled. I didn't want to go. And how could that be?

Will was a vampire—the walking undead, a fiend similar to the ones I'd vowed to kill. He'd been controlling my behavior, which explained much. I should want to be away immediately and never see him again.

"How did you find de lady?" Will asked Nurse.

"'Twas easy. The boy, Jamie, followed her daily. I followed him, and—"

"I followed you."

Everyone turned.

Reginald stood in the doorway.

Chapter Forty-two

"But love is blind, and lovers cannot see the
pretty follies that themselves commit."

—*The Merchant of Venice* (Act II, scene 6)

"Stop that!" Kate snapped.

Until she did, Will had not realized he'd been growling.
His fangs were out.

"Puppies," he muttered.

"What?" Kate asked.

"Nothing." Will did his best to imagine sweet baby dogs
gamboling about on spring green grass, and an instant later,
praise the saints, his fangs slid out of sight. He had no desire
to explain them to Kate's husband.

Kate's husband.

Will wanted to kill him. Perhaps—

No. He did not kill humans. Or at least he hadn't for a
very long time.

"What are you doing here, with him, in that—that—" The
man's lips curled beneath his unfortunate—was that a mole?—
nose. "Costume?"

"Acting."

He stared at her up and down, taking in what was left of her dress and the breeches that clung to her legs. "Like a whore, I trow."

"Sirrah," the Queen snapped.

Reginald glanced in her direction, then fell to the floor. "Your Majesty."

"I owe your wife much. I would not have her treated ill."

"Of course not, Your Majesty." The words came out muffled, his mouth pressed to the planks.

"Oh, get up!" The Queen flicked a pale, ringed hand. Reginald scrambled to his feet. "Barons do not grovel. Much."

"Barons?" he breathed. He wasn't as dumb as he appeared. *Unfortunately.*

"Yes. Now run along."

He bowed, then fastidiously brushed zombie ashes off his coat. At least he had the good sense not to ask what they were. "Katherine." Reginald snapped his fingers. "With me."

The Queen's mouth pursed. "Not so fast. She will come by and by."

The man hesitated. He wanted to do as the Queen ordered, but he didn't want to leave Kate behind.

"My lady, you must come home now." Nurse appeared at the top of the stairs, wringing her bony hands. "Think of the babe."

"God's spleen," Kate muttered, looking at the floor.

"Babe?" Reginald squeaked, looking at Kate's too-thin waist.

"Babe?" the Queen murmured, looking at Will.

"Damn," Will said, looking at Kate just as her husband's palm connected with her cheek.

Will snarled and jumped across the space separating them,

picking the man up with one hand around his throat, then slamming him into the wall. His head connected with a satisfying *thunk,* and Will thought about *thunking* him again.

But Nurse shrieked and fell upon Will's back. Kate got her elbow around the woman's neck and dragged her, kicking and screaming, free.

The Queen watched it all, the calm amid the storm. When she spoke, everyone froze. "Enough!"

Her face was white, her red lips tight; her eyes blazed as her father's had once done. All those in the room feared for their heads.

Except Will. He no longer cared if he lived or died. Without Kate, life was death anyway.

"Release them," the Queen ordered.

Kate and Will did as they were told, though neither of them was happy about it. Will gave Reginald one more sharp *thunk* first. The man glared evilly but moved out of Will's reach as quickly as he could.

"I know it cannot be mine," Reginald said. "Is it his?"

"No," Kate blurted. "He can't—"

"Oh, he can, and he has." Reginald pulled at what was left of his hair. "You imbecile. He's married. Keeps his wife and three children in the country. Did you think you could run away together and be happy ever after?"

Will wanted to groan. He wanted to shriek. He wanted to rip Reginald Dymond limb from limb. Certainly, Will was married, but it wasn't as it sounded. He would have explained things to Kate eventually.

Perhaps.

Or perhaps not. Because to explain about Anne and the

282 + Lori Handeland

children would have meant telling the truth about Will Shakespeare, and that he had never done.

"There is no babe," Kate said softly.

"Of course there is," Reginald began. "Nurse said—

"Nurse is a fool," Kate snapped. "I told her there was a child so she would leave me alone for one blessed instant. I told her she had the plague for the same reason."

Since Kate was now shouting, Nurse was able to hear. The woman began to cry.

"God's earwax," Kate said, and then she walked out.

Will took one step after her, and Reginald tensed, even as the Queen murmured, "Ah-ah-ah!" waving a finger adorned with an emerald large enough to choke a hound. "You will stay." She pointed at Will. "They"—she flicked that finger toward Reginald and Nurse—"will go."

The two began to leave, but the Queen murmured, "One last thing."

They turned back.

"There will be not a scratch upon your wife, Mr. Dymond. Do we understand each other?"

Reginald nodded, but his face had gone crimson.

Will opened his mouth to point out that the worst wounds were often located where no one could see, and the Queen spoke again. "You, Nurse, will ascertain there is a mark upon her nowhere, or I will know why. Do *we* understand each other?"

Since the Queen was shouting, Nurse bobbed a curtsy and said, "Yes, madam."

"Begone." The Queen waved her hand, turning away before they'd even begun to move. She knew they'd go when she said go. Everyone did.

Her dark gaze returned to Will. "And pray what shall we do about you, Master Shakespeare?"

"Whatever you wish, Your Majesty." Will sighed. "I care not."

"Oh, stop!" She clapped her hands, the sound making Will jump. "Do not be so morose."

"I am a vampire, Your Majesty. An undead fiend."

"I saw nothing fiendish." She glanced around. "Well, mayhap I did, but there are times when meeting fiend with fiend is necessary."

All Will could think of was that he'd lost Kate. He would never again see her, hear her, touch her. "Kill me if you like, Your Majesty," he murmured, staring out the door through which Kate had disappeared. "I will not hold a grudge."

Elizabeth snapped her fingers in front of his nose. "Shakespeare!" When his eyes met hers, those clever lips curved. "You risked your love to save me. Do you believe I would repay that gift with death?"

"It does not matter. Your wish, dear Queen, is my command. Wish me to die, and I will walk into the morning sun come tomorrow. You will not have to kill me. I will gladly do it myself."

"I see now why your tragedies are so tragic." She shook her head. "I discovered at a young age to find a bright side and hold on to it. If I hadn't, I would have jumped from the roof of one of my prisons long before I became Queen. But Queen I did become, Master Shakespeare." She reached for his arm, and being a gentleman, he gave it to her. "Walk with me, and I will tell you first how to woo back a lady you think is lost."

Will's head came up. The Queen's smile brought hope to his dead heart. "And then?"

She patted his hand. "Then I will tell you what it is that I wish from you."

Chapter Forty-three

"The true beginning of our end."
—*A Midsummer Night's Dream* (Act V, scene I)

I was mad, sad, tired, exhilarated, scared, victorious.

In a word—confused.

Did I love Will? I did not know. How could I love a blood-sucking, undead liar?

But I knew I did not love Reginald. Never had, never would. And I could not, would not, share his bed. The very thought nauseated me.

What was I to do?

I went home. Where else would I go? To my father? He'd send me right back.

I took off the filthy, torn costume, washed the ashes and the blood from my skin. Then I slipped into my nightgown and began to brush my hair. I'd never felt more alone in my life.

When Reginald stepped into the room, I felt even lonelier. "You disgust me," he said. "A common poet."

"Playwright," I corrected, "and hardly common."

I was defending him. I couldn't seem to help myself.

"You will live in this room. You will leave when I say; you will *do* as I say."

I bit my tongue. It would help nothing to argue. I had little choice.

Certainly I had a calling, but there was no money in zombie hunting. I could leave this house; I could kill enough tibonage to fill an ocean with ashes, but I would still starve in the streets soon enough.

Reginald left my room, and the lock clicked behind him. Silence descended. I went back to brushing my hair.

My gaze lit on the balcony doors, which Reginald appeared to have forgotten about. Stupid man. How did he think I'd made my escapes in the past?

I did not believe I would sleep, but the stress of the day overtook me, and in no time I dreamed of walking through a cool night fog. Nounou strode out of the mist.

Bébé, Nounou said. *Did you learn nothing from what I taught you?*

"I am the best chasseur in the land."

You are de only chasseur in de land, Nounou pointed out.

"Which does not make me any less the best."

Nounou's teeth flashed in her dark, smooth face. *So smart and yet so stupid.*

I stiffened. "What are you trying to say?"

You miss me, yes?

"More than I've ever missed anyone or anything."

In Haiti, I would be considered a bokor, *a sorcerer. Some might burn me. Dere are places in dis world, bébé, where some might burn you.*

"Your point?"

You do what you do because you have no choice. So does he.

"He, who?" I asked, but I knew.

Love is precious. Do not t'row de man away.

"He is not a man," I said.

No? You would say your Reginald—Nounou's lips curled as if she'd smelled something foul—*is a man, but Will Shakespeare is a monster?*

She had a point. Reginald was more of a monster than Will could ever be.

T'ink, Nounou said. *What is life wit'out love?*

"Death," I muttered.

Close enough.

And then I was back in my bed, awakening to the trill of a nightingale. Nounou was gone. Had she been a dream or a ghost? Did it matter?

When I stepped outside, the garden was cool and glowed with the light of the moon. Shadows danced here and there, but none of them were man-shaped. I waited for the call of that nightingale, but I'd only been hearing what I wished to hear.

"Ay, me," I sighed, and leaned upon the banister.

Will Shakespeare stepped into the silvery light. "Shall I hear more, or shall I speak at this?"

"If they see you, they *will* murder you," I whispered.

"There lies more peril in your eyes than twenty swords. If you want me dead, then 'tis dead I want to be."

I bent down, peering through the slats at Will below. "I would not for the world they saw you here."

Hope lit his face. "And but thou love me, let them find me here. My life were better ended by their hate, than death postponed wanting of thy love."

"You are a fool, Will Shakespeare."

"I have been called worse."

"No doubt." I was smiling. I was a bigger fool than he.

"Dark Lady, may I ascend?"

I straightened and stepped back. He took the movement for the invitation it was and climbed the trellis in a trice. He had no need any longer to appear human before me. I knew that he was not.

"Why have you come?" I asked.

"I had to make certain he would not hurt you."

"He dares not."

"The Queen?"

"And my rapier," I muttered.

Will choked on what sounded very much like a laugh, and I stifled my own smile. I would miss this. I never laughed or smiled with anyone like I laughed and smiled with him.

But another thought sobered me instantly, and though I should not care, I could not help it. "The Queen knows what you are, Will."

His smile bloomed. "Which is why she wants me to work for her. Considering there is at least one vampire loose in London—"

"The one that made Nigromante," I said.

Will nodded. "She thought having an undead fiend on her side might be a good idea."

"She has forever been a very clever queen."

Silence settled between us, at once companionable and uneasy. There was much yet to be said. I did not know where to start.

"You're married," I blurted.

Maybe I did know where to start.

"As are you."

"You knew that when you met me. You lied—"

"I never lied about Anne. I did not tell you of her, true,

but I did not say Will Shakespeare was unmarried. I would not, Kate."

"You said you could not have children, then—" My voice broke.

"They are not mine," Will said quietly.

I started, my eyes near bulging out. "What say you—?"

"They are Will's."

"But . . . you are Will."

He took a deep breath, let it out, and his shoulders slumped. Then he seemed to come to a decision, and the words flowed free.

"I once found a man by the side of the road. He had been robbed and left for dead. I gave him the choice to become like me, but he did not want to be undead, and I did not blame him. Instead, he gave me his life, his name, his wife, and his children. I swore to take care of them for the rest of their days. And I have." His lips tightened. "I will."

"She is not truly your wife? You have never—"

"Never," he assured me.

"Does she know? That you aren't . . . he?"

"Of course. I resemble the man greatly, but a woman knows."

"She does not mind?"

"She is the wife of Will Shakespeare. She has her children, a house, and no husband to annoy her daily."

I could understand that. Unless the husband was Will— *this* Will. I would be heartbroken if he never came home.

And it was then I understood the truth. I must be with him or die.

"My life were better ended," I murmured, "than death postponed wanting of thy love."

"Yes," Will agreed. "*Yes.*"

"Do you love me?"

"More than anyone in my lives."

"And do I really love you?"

Confusion dropped over his face. "I can't answer that, Kate."

"Did you *make* me love you?"

"No!" He took my hands in his, and they felt so good there, so right, I nearly missed his next words. "I can only make people act or forget. I can't make them feel something they do not. As far as I know, no one can."

"So this is real?" I whispered.

He kissed me—long and sweet and deep. His taste was danger—spice and fire and ice. His touch home—gentleness and warmth and love.

Will lifted his lips from mine. "What do you think?"

"If this is not real, I much prefer false," I said, and he laughed.

"Shh!" I glanced over my shoulder.

"Kate." Will put a finger beneath my chin and turned me to him. "He cannot murder me."

"He can try," I muttered.

"But he will not succeed."

"He will make my life a living hell." I laid my palm against Will's cheek. "More so now that I know what heaven is."

"We cannot go on like this," Will said.

"I do not know how to change it."

"I have a plan." Will pulled a small, dark bottle from his pocket. "Tomorrow night be certain to lie alone."

"Oh, I will be certain," I said. I planned to be certain of that for the rest of my days.

"Do not allow Nurse to lie with you in your chamber."

"I never do." The woman snored.

"Take this vial." He pressed it into my hand. "Go to bed, and of this distilled liquor drink. Through your veins shall run a cold and drowsy humor. Your pulse will cease. No warmth, no breath, will testify that you live. The roses in your lips and cheeks shall fade to pale ashes. Each part deprived will become stiff and stark and cold and appear like death."

Will tapped the bottle; the magic liquid danced. "And in this borrowed likeness of death, you will continue two-and-forty hours, then awake as from a pleasant sleep."

"But Reginald—" I began.

"In the morning comes to rouse you from your bed, and you are dead." Will lifted his brows. I was beginning to see the genius of this plot. "In your best robes on the bier, you will be borne to the same ancient vault where all the Dymonds lie. In the meantime, I will come and watch you wake and we will away. This, sweet Kate, will free us from our present trouble. What think you?"

I considered all he'd said, went over everything forward and back. "It seems the perfect plan." I spread my hands wide. "What could go wrong?"